Books by Pierre Schneider

Louvre Dialogues

Louvre Dialogues

by Pierre Schneider

Translated from the French
by Patricia Southgate

NEW YORK *1971* *Atheneum*

Several of the chapters in this book were originally
published in the French magazine *Preuves,* as well as
in *Art News, Art in America, Encounter, Cuadernos,* and
Der Monat.

Library of Congress catalog card number 72–135572
Published simultaneously in Canada by McClelland and Stewart Ltd.
Manufactured in the United States of America by
Kingsport Press, Inc., Kingsport, Tennessee
Designed by Harry Ford
First Edition

A Note to the Reader

This book consists of a series of conversations with artists at the Louvre. The lesson, if any, should emerge gradually, unsolicited. I shall do my best (it may well prove insufficient) not to draw conclusions. It seems useful, however, to indicate what led me to undertake the experiment.

Has the art of our time, which rejects all its predecessors, broken forever with the past? Can this abyss still be bridged by some sort of dialogue? And if a continuity still exists, what is its nature? I hoped that the confrontation between living artists and the art of the past could provide at least the beginnings of an answer to questions such as these. I also expected the encounter to throw light on the way those who are involved in the arts more actively than the rest of us see them. Finally, it occurred to me that my companions, absorbed in the task of trying to say what the works they were looking at meant to them, could unconsciously provide us with truer revelations about their own than the usual prepared studio statements.

The conversations are but the raw materials of the essays in this book. The words spoken should be viewed as the fragmentary, surviving islands of a mental universe swallowed by silence, which I have attempted to conjecture, as one seeks to reconstruct the sunken parts of Atlantis. In order clearly to draw the line between evidence and interpretation, and to make it easier for the text to glide from conversation to comment, from reflection to event, I have reserved the use of italics for the sayings—untampered—of my interlocutors.

With four exceptions, the artists themselves were kind enough to make drawings for use in this book. The drawings of Alberto Giacometti and Sam Francis were specifically chosen by them for the text; Barnett Newman and Bram Van Velde likewise selected their lithographs. Saul Steinberg's illustrations were partly chosen from previously existing work and partly drawn by him for the text.

Contents

Illustrations

Louvre Dialogues

The Louvre A Preface

> *I am waiting until we are at the Louvre before answering you. One can only speak properly about painting in front of paintings.*
>
> PAUL CÉZANNE

One rainy Sunday, Lucien Guitry suggested to his wife that they go to the Louvre. "What! Again?" she cried. He had not taken her there for fifteen years.

The first interpretation that comes to mind, of course, is that the poor woman was traumatized with boredom that day. I prefer a second: the experience had been so intense that it seemed to her to have happened only yesterday. Other museums as rich and interesting do exist, but there is a special magic about the Louvre. When I got the idea, a few years ago, of visiting it in the company of various painters and listening to the remarks they made about the works exhibited there, I prepared myself for more than one negative response. There were none. Would I have been as happy had I suggested that they come with me to the Uffizi, to the Metropolitan Museum or the National Gallery? Fantin-Latour sums up the painters'

opinion: "The Louvre, the Louvre, it's everything!"
And this was also Cézanne's opinion: "It seems to me
that everything is in the Louvre, that everything can be
loved and understood through it." A magical place because it is not a museum, but the Museum.

And it is the Museum because it embodies, to a large
extent, something other than a museum. A place to
take a walk, a meeting place. "I have a lot to tell you
and explain to you," Baudelaire wrote his mother on
December 16, 1847. "A letter is harder for me to write
than a book. Also, I loathe everything about your
house and especially your servants. I wanted to ask you
today to be at the *Louvre, at the Museum, in the big
Salon Carré,* at whatever time you indicate, but as early
as possible. The Museum, by the way, only opens at
eleven. It is the best place in Paris to have a talk; it
is heated, you can wait there without getting bored,
and besides it is the most proper meeting-place for a
woman."

The same Salon Carré had served as the setting for
Napoleon's marriage to Marie-Louise. The bridal train
proceeded there from the imperial residence, the Tuileries, passing through the entire length (422 meters)
of the gallery along the water, better known as the
Grande Galerie. Although full of art treasures (Napoleon had stuffed it with masterpieces confiscated
from conquered Europe), the Grande Galerie was
really nothing but a passageway between two royal
residences, one in the city, the other in what was then
the country: the Louvre and the Tuileries.

The Louvre had had a colorful record before becoming a museum. It had housed the first newspaper
published in France, a tapestry factory, the Académie
Française and its younger sisters the Academies of
Painting and Sculpture, the Stock Exchange, a gun-
powder factory, political clubs, revolutionary meetings,
electoral assemblies . . .

Above all, the Louvre had been lived in. Since the Middle Ages, it had served as the secondary, then the principal residence of the kings of France. Like every house, it—as well as the objects inside it—was functional and familiar. It lost this privilege when Louis XIV transferred the court to Versailles, but something of its original purpose still impregnated its walls, which the slightest thing could reawaken. The Revolution of 1848 remade the Louvre into a palace: the Palace of the People. The insurgents bivouacked in the Grande Galerie and drank from Greek and Roman vases. In so doing, they did not prove to be less respectful—not a piece was broken—than Degas, who owned an El Greco he sometimes hung his pants on. Such casualness is the mark of a utilitarian, living relationship. A bad painter said to him one day:

"Paintings are luxury items."

"Yours, perhaps," Degas answered. "Ours are staple commodities."

Good paintings do not make the best pants-hangers, far from it. Degas was not unaware that on the whole painting is more of a luxury than a staple commodity. The inexorable way in which it slips from one into the other, epitomized in the journey leading from the painter's studio to the collector's apartment, was a veritable torture for him. We know that he let his paintings go only when absolutely forced to, and that he tried to get them back in order, he said, to correct them. Actually, was it not more a question of trying to revive a work that died the moment it no longer had a use, no longer was a partner in a dialogue? For the same reason, Bonnard once got thrown out of the Luxembourg Museum, which at the time was filling the role of the Museum of Modern Art: a guard caught him, paint box in hand, in the process of retouching one of his canvases.

What drives the artist to undertake such reworkings —often unfortunate—is less the search for perfection, which he knows is out of reach, than the knowledge that the life-giving relationship, the relationship of necessity, exists only between the work and its creator. Once a mug has been made, anyone can drink from it; it is modeled, to some degree, on its function. This happy state of innocence˙is the birthright of handicrafts and industries.

The painter lives in the age of the experience. His work has no function. More exactly, it stopped having one the day the artist differentiated himself from the artisan—a divorce which is not simply that of the utilitarian object and the image, because for a long time the image itself was such an object: a vase into which the divine poured itself, a door opening onto the spiritual world, a mask of the invisible. The image dissolved into the religious experience toward which it oriented the user as the cup disappears in the act of drinking. It was also décor, sumptuous array, setting for the mighty of this world. Its meaning was given it by the priest, the prince. It was transitive.

During the Renaissance, art broke away from the gods, then ceased bowing to the commands of princes. From a means, it became an end; from transitive, intransitive. Around the image the protective and separating barrier of the frame appeared. For the individual genius, what a victory: to create not only the vessel but also the wellspring! There are few modern painters, however, who do not share the regret one can sense in Degas: because, in becoming an end, the work grows denser, more opaque. As our hand seems disproportionate, monstrous to us when our attention focuses on it—which happens when an illness or an accident immobilizes it—the modern image sometimes seems, all of a sudden, ponderous, absurd, tedious. Every organ is hideous unless redeemed by its function (Degas also noted that trees would be horrible if they did not shiver) .

Painting had stopped serving a purpose: as a result, one could see it too clearly, and one could see nothing but it. Ceasing to be operative, it tended to reduce itself to an object (of culture, of speculation), a body that life had deserted, to be collected in those "graveyards," those "morgues" which museums are for so many writers. There, the weight of their fixity can only be borne by the no less unnatural fixity of our attention, or by a hasty and distracted glance. Painting since the Renaissance has caused the rise of the consumer that suits it: the tourist.

And yet, a painting dwindles into an art object less in a home than in a museum. There, it participates in the general atmosphere. Surrounded by useful objects, it almost seems useful itself. Seen a thousand times, it ceases to be visible. The subtle web woven by the daily comings and goings in the place finally coats this foreign body, attenuates its shocking brightness. The unconsciousness and innocence which characterize the relationships of necessity envelop it in their warm folds, and from then on its heterogeneous nature recalls itself to our attention only unexpectedly, like an iceberg suddenly rising out of a tranquil sea.

That is why modern painters love the Louvre. It was a palace before being a museum: art lived there as much as it was on display. There lingers in it a sort of echo of the transitivity, the transparency lost and, again, dreamed of. It was in 1790 that the Louvre—at least, the Salon Carré—officially became a museum, but that was less a case of mutation than of long evolution. Leonardo da Vinci died at Amboise in 1519, leaving the contents of his studio, in particular the MONA LISA, SAINT ANNE and SAINT JOHN THE BAPTIST, to Francis I. Thus, the king who started work on the palace also set in motion the process that would eventually turn it into a museum. For these paintings of Leonardo's no longer were works integrated into a décor: they were

foreign bodies, meteorites, high in density and rare,
fallen into the space of the dwelling—art objects, collector's items. An automobile becomes a collector's
item the moment it no longer functions: the collector
is a King Midas who turns all the works he touches
into art objects. However, they lend themselves with
varying enthusiasm to this alteration: certain ones have
been constructed in such a way that they could never
have functioned in any case. Da Vinci, the Renaissance
man, corresponds to the collector, himself a product of
the Renaissance; the desire to create, through pure genius, a world outside the natural world demands for its
flowering an ideal space which the collection invents
and the museum perfects.

The paintings left by Leonardo to Francis I, the
initial core of the royal collections, formed a cancerous
cell in the organism of the palace. It proliferated rapidly. Louis XIII's dream was décor rather than collection. He wanted to transform the Grande Galerie into
a ballroom and called Nicolas Poussin back from Italy
to execute his plan. "I never understood what the King
wanted of me," Poussin wrote. It was simple enough,
but Poussin, in whose eyes painting was a world unto
itself, could not tolerate being forced to integrate it
into an environment.

Poussin would have found more understanding in
Cardinal Mazarin. Before moving into his own palace,
he had lived in the Louvre. Since the collector's quarters are the embryo of a museum, it was in Mazarin's
apartments that a section of the Louvre for the first
time shifted from an arrangement for living to an arrangement for viewing. Indeed, Mazarin was already
experiencing the anxieties of a museum curator. Chris-
tina of Sweden had asked to see his collection, and
Mazarin, away at the time, wrote his superintendent,
Colbert: "Do not let that madwoman into my private
rooms at the Louvre, because she might take my little
paintings."

Of all the legacies Mazarin left to Louis XIV, the most valuable was his collaborator Colbert, who assembled the royal collections in the Louvre. Amounting to about 200 works at the beginning of the reign, they numbered 2,000 at its end. (Today, the Louvre owns more than 25,000 works, among them 5,000 paintings, of which 2,000 are on exhibition.) Historians have often speculated about the Sun King's reasons for emigrating to Versailles. To all appearances, he was forced out by the paintings and statues. One cannot live in a museum. Fresh from his Parisian experience, Louis XIV saw to it that the museum cancer did not infect his new residence: the masterpieces of his collections were not incorporated into the Versailles décor at all, but remitted to the Department of Buildings, where people could study, and even borrow, them.

The Louvre officially became a museum only in 1793, more than a hundred years after the transfer of the court to Versailles. Before that could happen, Citizen Barrat had to cry before the Assembly, in 1791: "The Louvre must be restored and made into a famous museum." The principle of such a transformation was adopted the following year at the suggestion of the painter David. He was reviving a project dear to the hearts of the Encyclopedists. In the article "Louvre" in the *Encyclopedia,* Diderot suggested grouping the royal collections there and, in particular, giving the Grande Galerie, then occupied with relief maps of the royal fortresses, back over to paintings. Inspired by this advice, the Duke of Angivilliers, in charge of Beaux-Arts under Louis XVI, had already ordered a study for the renovation of the Grande Galerie, with an eye to providing it with overhead lighting. Plans, counterplans . . . time passed. In 1793, Hubert Robert painted a picture of a modernized Grande Galerie, which was still just a dream. He also painted a second version, immediately afterward, of the same subject in which the Grande Galerie, reduced to the state of decay, assumed the majestically melancholic air of the ruins of Caracalla, as if to point out to us that once life has fled, there are no alternatives but the museum or disintegration.

The Louvre had taken the latter road after the court's departure. A sea of slums grew up around it. The neighborhood became notorious and dangerous. Garbage rained down on the heads of passers-by. Under Louis XV, there was talk of demolishing it, but Madame Pompadour came to its rescue.

This period, although far from a glorious one, saw the establishment of the intimate relationship which links artists with the Louvre to this day. In effect, after having been the palace of the kings of France, the Louvre became a sort of Bateau-Lavoir.* Painters and sculptors moved in, living and working on the Grande Galerie mezzanine. They took all kinds of liberties with the illustrious building, for example, running chimney pipes through the noble beams and beautiful windows. Coypel, Desportes, Boucher, Chardin, Vernet, Greuze, David—all the art of the eighteenth century was domiciled at the Louvre. Visiting back and forth, chatting during chance encounters in the hallways, they formed a veritable community. The atmosphere must have been particularly joyful during the time of Hubert Robert, whose temperament had nothing of the melancholy of his ruins and whose art student's pranks often took a sporting turn (he nightly scaled Rome's Colosseum by its exterior façade), and of his friend Fragonard. Not even the storms of the Revolution could sour the carefree humor of "Petit Papa Frago." At the news that the pension Louis XVI had granted him had been reduced by two-thirds, the old painter jumped with joy.

* The Bateau-Lavoir was a ramshackle building in Montmartre where Picasso lived and worked in the early days of Cubism. A score of poets and painters connected with Cubism joined him there.

"Are you crazy?" his wife asked him.

"No, I am happy."

"Happy! What worse thing could have happened to us?"

"They could have taken everything."

Perhaps it was Fragonard's candle that Napoleon saw burning in the Grande Galerie one night in 1805 or 1806 as he passed the Louvre. In 1802, he had ordered the old palace to be taken away from the artists and turned over to art. Furious at not having been obeyed, the Emperor had them chased out forthwith. Fragonard, Vien, Lagrenée, Vernet, Robert, David—some two hundred artists were thus evicted.

This banishment marks the actual birth of the Louvre Museum. It was, in fact, the museographic act *par excellence.* It fulfilled the secret wish of all curators: that art dispense with artists. Not generally having Napoleon's dictatorial powers at their command, they fall back on symbolic forms of ostracism, such as the substitution of concepts for the individual creator: it is the style, the *Zeitgeist,* the school or the structure which engenders the work.

The artists' dream is otherwise. Cézanne, before Courbet's ROES' HIDEOUT, hanging above Ingres' THE APOTHEOSIS OF HOMER, cried: "You can't see a thing. It's so badly hung. When will they put a painter, a real one, in charge of the Louvre?" In a reflex common in the nineteenth century, Cézanne placed the Golden Age in the future, when it belonged to the events of the past. It was actually artists who were charged by the kings with the business of establishing and administering their collections. Francis I sent Andrea del Sarto to Rome, provisioned with funds, to collect "antiques": the Florentine Mannerist pocketed the money and stayed in Italy. This distressing experience did not prevent Louis XIV from entrusting the care of his private collection of paintings to Charles Le Brun and that of his drawings to Coypel. Until the advent of Napoleon, curators—*"concierges,"* as they were called then—were chosen from the ranks of painters. One of them, the playful Lépicié, thus came to edit the first *Catalogue Raisonné,* in 1752. Hubert Robert, named to the post in 1784, participated in the plans for renovating the Louvre. At David's instigation, he was named a member, with Fragonard, of the Commission that saved the masterpieces endangered by the Revolution. Artists enjoyed favored treatment in the days of royalty. Once a year, they exhibited their work at the Salon. (Unlike the living quarters, which moved from east to west, the Salon moved from west to east the length of the Grande Galerie, finally settling in the Salon Carré.) When the Revolution, with its passion for decimals, replaced the week with the *décade,* two days were reserved for cleaning and the work of the museum commissions, three days for the public and five days for the artists. These are privileges that are hard to forget. Even today, every artist entering the Louvre assumes the air of a monarch regaining his throne after long years of exile. To a guide who offered him his services, Toulouse-Lautrec, accompanied by friends from the Ecole des Beaux-Arts, replied:

"What for? We are the ones who make the Louvre!"

In a double sense. Not only does the artist provide the museum with new works: in his presence—and in his presence alone, we might be tempted to say—the ancient works continue to live, or, in other words, do not become petrified into objects of culture and admiration. The virulence of painting from the past, once a painter looks at it, is so strong that Ingres ordered his students, who had to pass the paintings of Rubens' which he detested in order to get to the canvases of the divine Raphael:

"Put on blinders!"

The only non-artist visitor, during the nineteenth

century, on whom the paintings in the Louvre had a comparably violent effect was the little prostitute celebrated by Baudelaire as *"la mendiante rousse."* She went there for the first time with the poet, who reports that, blushing, she covered her face at the sight of the nudities on view.

After 1848, the Salon was no longer housed in the Louvre; nevertheless, the latter continued to serve as a salon for French painters. It was there that Manet met Fantin-Latour, who was copying Venetian works to learn the secrets of color and who, in turn, introduced him to the Morisot sisters. It was also there that Manet came across a young man endeavoring to engrave one of Velásquez' infantas directly onto a copper plate and exclaimed:

"What nerve!"

The young man was Degas. The break with tradition effected by Manet in no way put an end to the close ties linking the modern artists with the Museum. It was at the Louvre that Manet first met the ragpicker Collardet, the model he used for THE ABSINTHE DRINKER, the first painting in which his personality asserts itself. Manet, one might object, still had one foot in the past. But what about his successors—Cézanne, for example?

Never was there a more assiduous, more passionate visitor to the Louvre. In his old age, he went there once a week. When he was away from Paris, he would pin photographs of his favorite canvases up on the wall— THE DEATH OF SARDANAPALUS by Delacroix, MARIE DE MÉDICIS LANDS AT MARSEILLES by Rubens. Untiringly, he kept coming back to Poussin's FLORA, hoping that she would reveal to him the formula he dreamed of for his own BATHERS.

Around 1900, the last bastions of tradition crumbled. It was a period, however, when Matisse, who was to bring modern painting out of its cocoon, lingered late at the Louvre with Marquet, searching for the "whites," the "holes" in the paintings, and wondering about the causes of these inert areas one finds even in the greatest masterpieces. As his teacher Gustave Moreau had sent his students there, Matisse would also send his own. Even after his pictorial revolution had been accomplished, he would go back there—and not only for mere pleasure. In 1909, he was working on his portrait of Greta Moll. The canvas had come to a standstill. "To console himself and to get new inspiration," his model recounts, "he went to the Louvre and we stopped work for a few days. There, he found the Veronese portrait. The lady in it was not wearing a white blouse, but her arms were placed before her the same way as mine, even though hers were heavier and more rounded. He adopted them for my portrait, which meant that, as usual, he had to change the whole painting. *It is getting to be of an incredible splendor!*' Now Matisse was satisfied."

The Louvre rarely opens its arms to a living artist in such a specific fashion. More often, it brings him a more general comfort, as Matisse himself would explain elsewhere: "You see, I was studying the things that attracted me, as in literature one studies certain authors before making up one's mind about one or another; above all, without wanting to learn their tricks, but for spiritual nourishment! I would go from a Dutchman to Chardin, from an Italian to Poussin." This procedure has the effect of removing the works from their biographical and historical contexts and reconstructing the anonymous conditions prevalent at the time when artists had the responsibility for the royal collections. "We have not attached any numbers," reads the notice accompanying the drawings exhibited at the Luxembourg in 1750, "nor the names of the artists, in order to give enlightened amateurs the opportunity to decide for themselves." And one can clearly see that it was still artists who made up the Commission charged with

hanging pictures in the Museum created by the Repub-
lic in 1791: "The arrangement we have adopted is that
of a bed of infinitely varied flowers. If, with a different
intention, we had showed the spirit of art in its infancy,
in its growth and in its latest stages . . . we would
have risked the well-founded reproach . . . that we
were shackling the minds of young students." The tur-
moils of the Revolution and the ruinous state of the
premises forced the authorities to close the recently
opened museum once more. By the time it reopened
its doors, in 1799, the paintings had been hung by
schools: the scholars had had their say over the painters,
history had triumphed over life.

The painter, reduced from then on to the role of
visitor, nevertheless has only to glance around the
works on view to reduce the historians' labors to rub-
ble. But what he causes to rise in their place is not life,
or rather it is a life different from the one at the historic moment when the artist was working—something
like a ground common to certain works belonging to
the most diverse periods and civilizations.

This affinity between a Fayum portrait and a portrait by Manet, for example, this coherence which resides outside history and even denies it, emerges only
against the background of time. Paradoxically, it is at
the heart of the scholars' Museum, with its schools, its
movements, its classified cultures, that the painter becomes aware of what does not belong to history. Caught
himself in the historical flux, he finds at the Museum
the revelation of a second possible belonging, which is
not the negation of time but its other side. The more
he feels himself to be the prey of the temporal, the
more he will search the Louvre for this other domain.
Cézanne visited it assiduously because he belonged to a
movement that, more than any other, was predicated on
the fleeting moment. Hence his anxious dream: "To
make of Impressionism something as solid and endur-

ing as museums." It is at moments of intense perplexity, of questioning, of innovation that painters return to the Louvre, as sailors dream of a port during a storm. It was, I believe, Picasso who wished, one day, to hang his canvases among the masterpieces in the Grande Galerie, to see if they "held up." Which is to say: to know if they, too, possess that character through which the great creations of all times are related and which, just like the public, they call beauty, disregarding the obscurity of the word, satisfied no doubt to find in it the glow of permanence evoked by Mallarmé: "I see nothing fade away which has been beautiful in the Past."

Mallarmé was mistaken: the beauty of paintings fades very fast, faster and faster. Standing before THE ENTRANCE OF THE CRUSADERS INTO CONSTANTINOPLE, Cézanne lamented: "It's terrible . . . might as well say that you do not see it. We no longer see it. I saw, I myself saw this painting die, pale, disappear. It could make one cry. From decade to decade, it keeps fading. . . . One day, there will be nothing left of it." Delacroix was haunted by this physical death of his work, but the methods he used to avert it—resorting to bitumens— only hastened the end (just as Quentin de La Tour killed his pastels by trying to fix them). *Ars longa, vita brevis,* the saying goes: for modern painting, the opposite is true. "At the Louvre, in Paolo Veronese's ESTHER," Fénéon wrote, "through the colonnades of the palace of Ahasuerus, one sees, to one's amazement, the white streets turn dull beneath an inky sky—once blue: that blue was fashionable." And he adds: "The painter who most clearly supervised the fabrication of his colors is precisely the one whose colors have blackened the most—Leonardo." As if real, material space wanted to take vengeance against an art which, through the magic of perspective, had replaced it with a fictitious, immaterial space.

There are obviously more expeditious methods of destruction. "Let's burn down the Louvre, then," Cézanne cried, "right now . . . if we are afraid of what is beautiful."

The painters were the first to raise the cry: "Burn down the Louvre!" From Pissarro and Manet to Picasso and the Futurists, artists have often preached the destruction of the Louvre—before they saw their own works hanging there. Cézanne himself, who states: "Yes, the Louvre is the book from which we learn to read," also recalls: "I used to want to burn the Louvre."

This revolt against the Museum is born of the sentiment, often ill-defined, that the past and the present are antinomic. To submit oneself to the dictates of history is to remove oneself from the creative instinct, from life. "Since we made museums to create masterpieces," Quatremère de Quincy noted in 1815, "there have been no more masterpieces to fill the museums." The denial of the museum is as natural as the child's revolt against its parents. Courbet visited the Louvre with his father, who asked him what he thought of the paintings they saw. "Next to mine," Courbet exclaimed in his Franche-Comtois accent, "all this painting is *merde!*" It might seem surprising that this brutal rejection was formulated by a painter who, after all, was the last great representative of the Tradition. But having contempt for one's parents does not imply that one challenges the laws of heredity. It is perhaps at the precise instant of the apparent break that the real chain is enriched by a new link.

The painters' museophobia has other causes. Every museum is a little like Madame Tussaud's. A painting put in a museum is a painting withdrawn from circulation; it is retired from the cycle of life and death. From being a work, it becomes an object. And what can one do with objects, except collect them? However public they may be, collections are none the less hoards.

Removed from the wall of a church or a bar, a fresco no longer speaks to us except in indirect discourse.

This absence of immediacy in art's relations with the public has weighed more and more heavily on painters as the necessity for direct discourse imposed itself on them—in short, since Edouard Manet. The pursuit of the present indicative implied the rejection of all inheritances—in other words, of the Tradition to which the Museum had assembled the testimonials. Another tie, a deeper one, existed between the Museum and the Tradition. They had been born at the same time and answered the same need. The intransitive art of the Renaissance called for an abstract space shielded from ordinary life as the canvas is separated from its material environment by its frame: the Museum answered this exigency. One could not shake the system elaborated by Giotto, Van Eyck and their successors without calling into question the place where sooner or later paintings came to rest, like men in a graveyard. "Life! Life! That was the only word on my lips. I wanted to burn the Louvre," said Cézanne.

He added: ". . . poor jerk that I was!" For in the meantime he had come to realize that the Museum, revealer of the general space into which all works of art dissolve, is also the guarantee of their individuality. The more personal a work of art is, the more it resists being integrated into an architecture. In their pure states, personality and decoration are incompatible. The Museum (the collection), which stands against the dilution of real life into space, appears as the frame, the true dimension of the individual. To destroy the one is to deny the other, which, since the Renaissance, would be equivalent to a mutilation.

Hence, the very ones who, in the nineteenth century, rediscovered two-dimensional space, which, reducing the work to its own surface, allows it to rejoin the surface of the walls and integrate with them—decoration:

mode of expression specific to real space—these same
ones refuse to renounce the depth, the identity of
things (and of themselves), although they insist on the
use of methods which make "a hole in the wall." While
he clearly perceives the contradiction of the two approaches, the modern painter refuses to limit himself
to one or the other. "Giotto, deliver me from Paris!
Paris, deliver me from Giotto," the young Degas wrote
in one of his notebooks. Manet longed for the silence
of paint and the eloquence of the subject matter at the
same time. Matisse struggled, his whole life long, to
reconcile Cézanne's depth with Muslim decorativeness.
It seems as if painters have actually sought after this
contradiction, as if they felt that modern space was
neither the flatness of reality nor the three-dimensionality of the fictitious, but that it must emerge from the
field defined by this new dilemma. Thus the problem
confronting certain painters, as early as 1860, strangely
resembles the one which many economists, sociologists
and philosophers consider to be the great question of
our times: how to reconcile the individual dimension
and the collective dimension?

Perhaps dualism will seem one day to be the essential character of the times. At any rate it illuminates the
ambivalent attitude of painters over the past hundred
years toward the Museum. One understands why they
are drawn to the Louvre, which has the flavor of a residence and a museum. And one understands equally that
the Museum, at once the incarnation and negation of
the space they dream of, seems alternatively to them to
be the supreme haven and fit to be burned to the
ground.

But the fire they speak of does not burn: it is art.
It must destroy, since it is nothing unless it is birth.
And so being, it rejoins everything which, before it,
has been birth. The history of the fire and the fire are
but one. Since I began this book, some of those who

were my revolutionary companions at the Louvre have become classics. Where an abyss appeared to be gaping, now there is evidence of a chain forged. In this place where the fire burns and does not burn, a painting finished yesterday could have been done at the time of the Pharaohs, while a Mesopotamian statue would not seem out of place in a contemporary studio.

The fire which in recent times has been threatening museums almost everywhere is less platonic. Groups crowding against the prudently closed doors, slogans painted on the walls or scratched into the canvases themselves, such as these words drawn by students on the PORTRAIT OF CARDINAL DE RICHELIEU by Philippe de Champaigne: "Let us divert art from its function of mortification. Art is dead, long live the Revolution!"

These are familiar themes in the aesthetic thought of the 1960s. Art is a mortifier (or a death) because it produces objects, and the only possible relationship with these objects is possession, which is the prerogative of the bourgeoisie, which has invented culture as the mode of valorizing objects of art.

This reasoning confuses the object and the work. The former is intransitive, an end. The latter is transitive, a means. The object is the depositary of a certain number of qualities, of values; whether we look at it or not, it remains unchanged. The work, on the contrary, is only fulfilled with the participation of the senses and the intelligence it solicits, demands from us. To be sure, the critique I have just outlined applies to the art which emerged during the Renaissance and tended to substitute the object for the work. But have we not specifically been endeavoring to reverse this tendency for the past hundred years and more—that is, precisely during the period that saw the triumph of the bourgeoisie? Better still, the artist who deserves the honor for this reversal was the most bourgeois of men: Edouard Manet.

For the current protestors, these nuances have no

interest. One would argue with them in vain that if Hitler proclaimed that 2 + 2 = 4, mathematics was not thereby discredited, or that no one has yet suggested destroying flowers and trees on the pretext that only the rich have gardens. Finally, if the object only asks to be collected, the work must be receptive. In order to be an object, a painting only needs its painter; to become a work, it further requires the collaboration of the viewer. If he neglects or refuses to participate, the image which was a "transparency," a threshold between an ordinary and a more exalted state of consciousness, is nothing but a piece in a collection. Not definitively, however: one disinterested glance will restore its transparency. To reject the Fayum portrait along with Benvenuto Cellini's cup because they both happen to be in a rich industrialist's collection is to forget the difference between the object and the work, a forgetfulness all the easier because what constitutes this difference—the active participation of the viewer—grows less and less perceptible to the minds of today, for which there are only literal truths. Light in art? Electric lighting. Motion in art? Moving parts. The participation of the former "spectator"? The act of pressing a button which lights or agitates the object. How could those who press the button with such enthusiasm understand that one can participate in a painting by an act of conscience on which one cannot put one's finger and that the participation offered them by kinetic manipulation actually is purely passive, infinitely closer to the blind gesture of the worker on an assembly line than to the anonymity of the Romanesque artisan freely expressing himself within the framework of a general *esprit?* How could they understand that the dynamic of a work does not reside in its being set in motion by some mechanism, any more than a painting depicting a stampede is necessarily more dynamic than one of chess players?

Literalism confuses the work with the object. Every work has an object for a substratum, as fire takes hold on wood. The function of the work is precisely to consume the object. The material density and the sum of the conventions, the meanings that make up the object vanish in the flames that they have fed. Fire which does not burn and must constantly be rekindled: if one day a certain painting that usually speaks to us suddenly refuses, it is because we have not done our work. On that day, the museum will just be a museum to us. The object is intolerable, like a dead body. And there is no other way for us to get rid of it except on the garbage heap: history, sociology, psychology and aesthetics will finish up what we have not been able to burn. But to deny work because it implies an object is to condemn men on the grounds that they are future corpses.

Abraham was about to sacrifice his son Isaac when the Lord ordered him to replace the child with a lamb. This substitution is the basic act which founds and defines civilization, because it means the end of the tyranny of the literal. Not only does it affirm that the wounding impact of things and of acts can be replaced by their symbols and simulacra, but, above all, since the equivalency is only established through the spiritual effort which brings together the separate natures of the signifier and the signified, it sets this effort at the heart of the system. The Lord laid down the terms of the equation, but the converter who establishes their relationship can only be man. Without poetic flight, the wine cannot replace the blood. Literalness is only abolished by an act of our conscience. From it alone springs the fire which burns and does not burn. It alone can recognize the truth of a painted image which is only an illusion, which escapes from history without ceasing to belong to it. For, of course, history exists and the fire burns and the object continues to weigh on us. Except in Abraham's sacrifice, renewed by every work of art. The day when this substitution will no longer be tolerated, we will stop going to the Louvre.

Joan Miró

"*We'll pretend that we're going to the coun-try, all right? There, you walk around, and the sun's too hot, so you sit down and ask a farmer's wife for a glass of milk. Otherwise, this place gets boring!*"

Miró is anxious, and, to tell the truth, I share his apprehension. For children and their escorts, visiting a museum is a chore. And have we not been told time and time again that what characterizes Miró is "the gift of childhood"? Imagination in close touch with the sub-conscious, mind that has trouble distinguishing reality from dream, proliferating experience uncensored by reason and unpruned by routine, ability to indulge in games (some forbidden) with intense seriousness, start-ling perspective that enlarges certain details and atroph-ies certain "important" parts because the eye that sees and the hand that renders the vision belong to one who barely comes up to the grownups' knees, sudden leaps from laughter to tears through the whole gamut of grimaces, and finally that jovial cruelty typical of the age we call tender and La Fontaine called pitiless. The temptation to interpret Miró's work in terms of child-hood is great indeed. Not the Countess of Ségur's image

23

of childhood, of course, but modern psychology's, which shows the child innocent not of crimes but of remorse, *pure* but pure as an undiluted poison. Miró: an adult talent serving a childlike world.

Such an interpretation reduces the work to an imagery of the marvelous, a series of droll or alarming vignettes, a peep show in which *l'humour noir* and *le drame rose* knock each other about. It strangely limits Miró's art: for what use is it to have been the first to have freed painting from the laws of gravity if renouncing gravity was the price that had to be paid? Is not such outrageous liberty precisely what we easily grant to people whose actions do not carry much weight? If this were the case, the confrontation I had asked Miró to submit himself to would have been, on my part, an error in judgment, a lack of taste, a breach of etiquette, and an unpardonable confusion of text and margin.

This had been my fear, having never seen more than a few of Miró's pictures at a time and being unable to compare the different periods of his work except with the aid of memory and of that printed memory: photography. The retrospective at the Musée d'Art Moderne, in 1962, upset my earlier impression of the Catalan painter, supplanting it without, however, repudiating it. The units, taken individually, were just as I remembered them, but from their sum a new quantity or, more precisely, quality emerged. Once it appeared, it abolished all that had preceded and prepared it, as the rise of the moon extinguishes the stars. Far from dis-

solving into the wealth of its own invention, as happens
when ingeniousness alone governs a work, the breath-
taking diversity of Miró's periods, the lightning succession, *sol y sombra,* of the episodes, do not add up to a
simple narative, a "comic strip"—now funny, now monstrous: they engender a new dimension which indis-
criminately devours humor, imagination, anecdote and
dream as well as reality. What name can we give to this
voracious thing? I remember the words that, to my surprise, came to my mind: gravity, solemnity. *It* was motionless, while the forms wriggled, twisted frantically
on the walls. Amid the superabundance of the pictur-
esque and the bizarre displayed before us, *it* was neutral,
anonymous. And upon reflection, I realized that *it* was
identical with the presence which emerged from the
plethora of the museum, swallowing up history and the
stories of generations just as, under my very eyes, at
the Palais de Tokyo, *it* devoured those of one man.
Miró says:

*"Actually, my painting is not opposed to what one
sees at the Louvre. Everything is linked."*

On the first day after his arrival in Paris, in 1918, he
had gone there.

*"I went every day, I wanted to see all the painting.
When I arrived in Paris, I was disoriented, paralyzed.
For three or four months, I was incapable of painting.
My companions went to work, quite naturally. But,
secretly, I was pleased by my incapacity: it proved that
I had been shaken up. Later, at the time when I was
painting Mrs. Mills' portrait, I used to come here every
afternoon. It helped me, by providing a shock, an opposition. What impressed me the most were those Dutch
interiors where you can see a tiny dot—tak!—like a
fly's eye. For me, that was the outstanding thing. It was
more than minuteness: it was the sharp point in a fairly
large canvas . . . sharp, luminous—a microbe's eye.*

"I was also attracted by force. Rembrandt, the impact

of power. After that, I would go back at certain times. Whenever I launched on a new venture, I would come to see the classics. But I never copied anything at all, except in Barcelona, when I was fourteen years old, and then I copied Urgell. Now that I have found my balance, I come to the Louvre less often. It is a need that I don't reason with."

I, whose function is to reason, tell myself that this grave resonance, while making our visit today seem more normal, only deepens the mystery of Miró's work. To the mutations abounding in his painting, above and beyond the phenomena of spontaneous generation, extravagant grafting, scissiparity, proliferation, compenetration, phagocytosis, one supreme one must be added: that which makes us forget all the others (and thereby also allows us to be interested in them). Metamorphosis is at work. The museum has time enough to kill time and displays so many styles, so many diverse subjects, that they end by canceling out one another. With Miró, the passage into the state of solemn abstraction is instantaneous, despite the visible presence of the concrete —the concrete in its most literal form. There must be, in every canvas, a precise point, a given moment—a fly's eye—where everything hangs in balance, where the path of playing hooky from school intersects the path of duty (since the museum is also made up of schools). Attention cannot waver from a single dot: that dot might be precisely the animal we were lying in wait for; he would jump and disappear before we could collect our wits.

Determining the conditions of this dizzying conversion of littleness into bigness is what, for my part, I was expecting from our visit to the Louvre, hoping that my companion's instinct, far from his habitual terrain, more sheltered from the dangers of his own creativity, would prove to be less nimble, less wary, and thus allow me to catch it in action.

Still, it was no easy task. He had given me warning: *"You know, I don't know how to talk. You will have to pay attention to what I do: when I scratch my nose, when I stop, when I nudge you with my elbow. And also, the ways in which I am silent."*

Miró's silences . . . No matter how well I know them and arm myself to escape their traps, they get the better of me. And no matter how hard I try, it is always I who break them. Miró also has words more silent than silence, such "proper" responses, impeccable! Thus the insect assumes the color of his surroundings, the better to conceal himself. Then, too, there are those words, those phrases which are ours but which (probably) do not mean the same thing when Miró uses them. Finally, if, like us, he is sensitive to influences and accessible to the outside world, it is not in the same way that we are. Like children listening to the grownups' conversation, he interprets it awry, according to his own bias: his reflections are deflections. In the infinite gamut of common experiences, he does not react to the same stimuli, nor in the same manner.

"I am not sensitive to the wind, to the temperature, to the rain or the sun," he says as dark clouds gather over the Carrousel, impelling us to talk about the weather. *"But I feel the phases of the moon."*

Thus what is true of Miró's work is also true of his words; they require more than an interpretation: a decoding. To provide the reader of a mystery story with a key to the enigma is to deprive him of the better part of his pleasure, is it not? Besides, am I sure that my key is the right one? Indeed, is a key really necessary? Have I imagined obscurities where all is candor? It will be best, therefore, to resist, if I can, the temptation to explain and classify, and simply to record Miró's words, deeds and gestures at the Louvre. The reflections they inspire in me, sometimes on the spot but more often upon reading over my notes, are dismissed until the end of this account, whence the reader, if he so desires, may dismiss them altogether.

Death, they say, puts things in their place. At any rate, the long hall lined with Roman sarcophagi succeeds in bringing order to the crowd jammed up before the entrance. Like officers rallying their troops after capturing a fortress, the guides attempt to marshal their groups after they gain admission. Miró comes to a halt at the sight of an arm, apparently without bodily connections, brandishing a piece of yellow paper above a sea of heads. And I am immediately reminded of the *membra,* no less alive for being *disjecta,* in my companion's paintings—for example, HAND CATCHING A BIRD,

I think . . . but I have resolved not to think. At the end of the hall, a slight pause. The beginnings of a traffic jam on the left (the VENUS DE MILO is in that direction) make us turn to the right.

Roman statues. Miró walks past them, looking worried, without a word until he spots a Fayum portrait of a woman—the one wearing a large jewel: *"That's a little like the Lady of Elche, don't you think?"* Another portrait, with a triangular head: *"Ah! That's beautiful."* He clicks his tongue like a child presented with an ice-cream cone. *"Like a little cat! And that look! That is a living, mysterious look, compared with the* MONA LISA! *And that mauve, almost like a Bonnard! And look at the design of those earrings: nothing but that"* (it is a sort of parabola, terminated at one end by three circles), *"enlarged, what a painting it would make!"* Another portrait, the model with Negroid features, rougher in execution: *"That is stronger than a Rouault."*

He puts on his glasses, takes them off, puts them on again, goes *tsk, tsk.* . . . *"The elongated nose, the close-set eyes, it reminds me of El Greco. I wonder why."* He freezes, petrified by attention. *"Ah, yes, he's squinting, there, that's it!"* Long silence. *"And what color, what plastic discipline!"* The portrait of a native woman reminds him of *"Catalan things, in the intensity, the folds, the volumes of the nose and cheeks."* Of the head of a native man: *"It's as strong, as brutal as a Negro sculpture."* And he adds, after looking around:

"A little room with nothing in it but this would be as imposing as a room of Vermeers or Corots. As a matter of fact, this grisaille is like Corot: minuscule things, but you can see everything in them."

Silence while we rapidly cross through the room of Roman sculpture. At the end, in a kind of anteroom, various Late Roman and Paleo-Christian fragments. Miró stops in front of a piece of mosaic bearing an inscription.

"What plastic discipline! I can't see it either larger or smaller. It is just right. What freedom, what discipline! If this mosaic is something minor, then major painting bores me, except Corot."

"Does your interest in this mosaic stem from the fact that it speaks to us?"

"No. Above and beyond all, it is the visual shock that counts. Afterwards, one wants to know what it says, what it represents. But only afterwards."

Miró says he is fascinated, as never before, by handwriting: *"Mine has changed, my signature, for example.*

*I feel like doing a series of canvases as black as a school-
boy's slate, of the letters of the alphabet—zak! zak!"*
The onomatopoeia is accompanied by the lashing gestures of a coachman. *"Take the date, March 5, 1963."*
He writes it with biting gestures in the air, prolonging
the verticals down to the ground in violent sword
thrusts—*zak.*

*"That earring we saw just now: the three pearls, tak,
tak, and zak! On a huge canvas. A simple line and a red
circle, as a final period. But how that period is placed!
With infinitesimal precision. You cannot move it a
hair's breadth. Yes, I used to do things like that before,
but from sensitivity, as if the line were breathing. Now
I am involved with something more brutal, like a dag-
ger thrust, like the letters in Henchir Msadiné's funeral
mosaic. Look: it has the precision of the architecture of
a book, it's made quite differently from 'handwriting.'
Now that I want to do a book, all these mosaics are a
lesson for me at the moment. Yes, the book excites me
more and more. It is a form of architecture. If everything is not in the right place, it collapses. Then, too,
I like working with artisans. Provided I don't take myself for a genius, don't give orders, but work with them.
I owe a lot to artisans."*

We have entered the room of mosaics from Africa.
Miró whistles with admiration in front of the PHOENIX,
nods his head. *"That is beautiful. There's nothing more
to be said, when you look at that."* But the PARROTS,
whose bodies are shaped like a whip—straight handle
and curved lash—make him say: *"Zak—and there you
are."* And in the tragic tangle of THE BATTLE OF THE

AMAZONS he draws my attention to a part of the mountain which begins in the shape of a nun and ends in an umbrella: *"Nothing but that, and make something monumental out of it, make a monument sixty feet high and put it in Place de la Concorde."* Before a mosaic found at Constantine, representing the Triumph of Neptune and Amphitrite, carefully, skillfully modeled, quite worthy of the Renaissance, he sighs: *"You can't breathe. It is like wearing a suit that's too tight, with a button in the wrong place."* And before THE RECLINING RIVER, a specimen of official Roman painting: *"It only seems right. But one could easily shift the figures around."* And after a long, oppressed silence: *"Let's go to my neighborhood."*

His neighborhood is Sumer. Hardly has he entered the first of the Mesopotamian rooms than he is intensely on the alert. *"Look,"* he says, quickening his step, *"look at that girl, the sack with that chain dangling from her stiff arm!"* Silence, until the arm is out of sight. *"In the past, I came to the Louvre chiefly for the paintings. Now, more and more, I come for this. Still, there is Corot. Daylight, a landscape by Corot. Tiny little strokes—ping! ping! ping!—in their right places. And the man's dignity. Where is dignity today? And his humility: he would not have minded remaining almost anonymous. Calm."*

Here, too, it is calm, silent, warmly anonymous. *"The slightest thing is beautiful here."* Miró suggests that we slip through the rooms quickly, without any set plan, leaving it to the works to stop us as we go by. Almost at once, that happens. Before the FOUNTAIN IN THE SHAPE

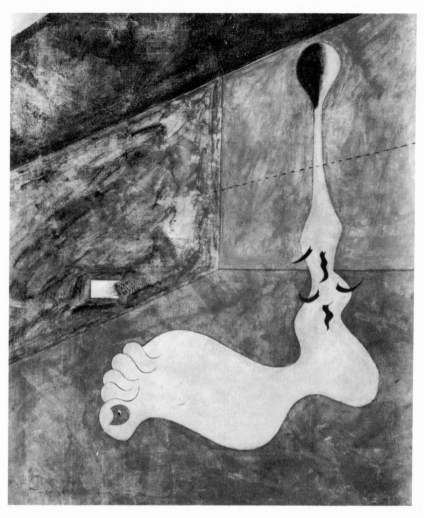

Joan Miró: LA STATUE

Mosaic: THE BATTLE OF THE AMAZONS

OF AN EAGLE (Tello) : *"Ah!"* His hand rises and falls again in a gesture of despair and admiration. At the sight of the PRINCE OF LAGASH (Gudea) : *"You can't hurry past this."* Babylonia, on the other hand, causes us to accelerate. *"Here, it's a different matter. The man says: I want this, I want that. You can feel it, and it bothers you."* We race down a staircase, climb up the opposite side and, suddenly, Miró freezes in front of five Carthaginian steles lined up on the steps like cacti.

"What a beautiful arrangement! Why is it in the stairway? Are they ashamed of it? It is minor art, I suppose. But next to it, what is major art?"

A detour brings us to the collection of Luristan bronzes recently bequeathed to the Louvre by M. Coiffard. Miró has already come to see them several times and, in truth, it is not astonishing that he should like them: do we not note the same strange hybridizations, the same grafts which—proof of the vitality of the cuttings—invariably "take" in his own work? *"Little things, but grand."* And before a small horse bit: *"It is like a Chinese signature."* We head for the exit between two rows of large Assyrian mythological beasts. *"These are less grand than one of those little bronzes."*

Outside, we pause, dazed.

"It's like getting off an airplane after an eighteen-hour flight. You no longer know what time it is, or where you are. How beautiful the sky is today!"

The next morning, we begin our second visit to the museum as soon as it opens, for Miró thinks that we went a little too fast the day before. When you do a thing, you must do it well—i.e., in depth. So here we are again among the cicerones sounding the call to arms. Remembering yesterday's episode, I point out to Miró that as early a painting as TILLED LAND contains human members which have chosen to live their own lives: feet, hands, eyes.

"*Yes,*" replies Miró, "*even as a child I was haunted by a hand, eyes, in flowers, in trees. I thought of plants as human beings. I had painted a* BOUQUET *with, at the tips of the stems, fragments of a face, an eye, a hand.*"

"And the feet?"

He thinks a long time, seriously.

"*No, no feet.*"

On our way back to the Chaldean section, he says:

"*My imaginary world is connected with life. At home, in the afternoon, I go for walks: it is reality that gives me the shock, the ideas. A wall, a pebble. The sign is a very alive thing for me, never abstract. I see this sign begin to move, it goes outside, it takes a walk on the Carrousel. The life of a work is just that: being able to take a walk. Up there, in the rooms full of painting, there are a lot of them that have never been for a walk.*"

Around us now, those civilizations that mark the beginning of history.

"*History makes no difference to me. A little Pompeian landscape and a Corot belong to the same time. The shock that illuminates me has nothing to do with time. Time does not exist for me.*"

As he talks, Miró's eye, taking advantage of the diversion, slips away and goes about its own business. A round eye, with such a piercing look that one would swear it was lidless. I have the impression that it belongs to someone other than the person conversing with me, who lifts his arm in a gesture of supplication, shakes his head, clicks his tongue, and cries before a glass case full of very small Tello objects from the end of the fourth millennium B.C.

"*Ah! Tremendous! Do they think of this as great art, or what? These little things, they fill an enormous room. How can you respond to paintings after you've seen these things?*" (Silence.) "*Art? They probably never even heard of the word.*"

"Do you think of it yourself—art, I mean—while you're working?"

"Me? (He bursts out laughing.) 'Artiste-peintre'!"

Although Miró admires everything here, it nevertheless seems to me that his predilection is for objects of bizarre shape, assymetrical, tattooed with inscriptions,
like the Tello shard on which is drawn the silhouette
of an elk: *"Incredible! A mural in which there would
be only this shape, what a thing that would be!"* And
the FOUNTAIN IN THE SHAPE OF AN EAGLE which had attracted us yesterday: *"This sort of butterfly-woman,
with her little eyes, what a marvel . . . that and the
colossal statue of Gudea."* For the admiring glance
jumps from the little terra-cottas to the great basalt
blocks, to that Tello statue of which only the lower part
survives: the robe of feathers and, in their niche, the

feet—*all alone, alive.* And also the statue of Manishinsu
(Susa) : *"Very moving. This block with those folds, like
rain pouring down it. Everything is in it: figure, landscape, you don't really know. An almost invisible fringe
on the huge architecture of the statue."* Before the
famous stele of Naroun-Sin, on the other hand, Miró
screws up his eyes, scratches his ear: *"You don't get that
little shock, as over there. It is too official."*

But again, how to report that essential element of our
dialogue: silence? Miró is at home with it, at least that
other Miró who commands the lidless eye. In attempt-
ing to understand him, only a few clues are at my dis-
posal: eyebrows more or less knit, shrugs of the shoulders, a more or less worried expression. Speech seldom
illuminates that other side. It is speech which interrupts

the silence, not the other way around. Prudent speech, controlled and obliging, out of kindness, of course, but also to forestall indiscreet intrusions.

We have reached the Egyptian section. As in Chaldea, writing clasps the harsh mass of the stone in its fine strands. *"After the cuneiform we have just seen, it seems dead. It smacks of ministries, of consulates."* Miró grows more surly by the minute, to the point where he becomes aware of it and makes a great effort at politeness. Before the stele of the Serpent-King (Thinite) : *"If we had started from this end, we would have stopped here. But after the Chaldeans . . ."* A thick column covered with hieroglyphics: *"The guys who carved this must have kept looking at their watches to see if it wasn't time to go and have a drink. . . . It's terrific, for the man who talks about Art."* We hurry on until we come to the CHANCELLOR NAKHTI frozen in his fold of wood (Middle Empire). *"Here we can stop for a few moments,"* he says, but it will be his last concession. Not even the great BEARER OF OFFERINGS (Twelfth Dynasty) will cheer him up: *"Pretty, but too refined."* And we start off again in a morose silence. It will only be broken when, again passing the foot of the grand staircase, Miró spies, in the vast, darkly vaulted, many-leveled storage area under the steps, a whole conglomeration of Roman busts, escalators, empty pedestals. *"Very mysterious, sheer Piranesi,"* he says, suddenly cheered. And instead of heading for the exit—we have been wandering around for three hours—he takes the grand staircase, against the tide of the crowd.

"All these people are going home satisfied: mission accomplished. They ought to be given a certificate at the exit."

The prospect of the rooms of French painting opens before us: a good half mile of canvases, as the crow flies, I would say. Miró rubs his hands together: *"It's doing me a lot of good, this visit to the Louvre. Especially be-*

cause with you we're doing it thoroughly." Since the head tires more quickly than the legs, I am relieved, after that, to have him suggest that we follow the method already applied to antiquity: to walk quickly, not looking for anything, and see what is capable of attracting our attention. Silence (which I fancy to be dismayed) before the great Salon pieces. At David's LEONIDAS: *"This is really a bit cruel, what we are doing!"* A pause, then: *"You need cruelty in life, or else you go dead."* Ingres, Girodet, Guérin, Chassériau, Courbet—*"Here we stop."* A statement of fact, for he has already halted in front of THE STUDIO. *"This nude woman has all the grandeur of the things we saw downstairs."* And as if he had been looking for nothing here except this vindication, at last, of our times, Miró suggests that we end our visit then and there.

"That was great, yesterday, going around at top speed like American tourists. And in spite of that, before Courbet, we were nailed to the spot. Zak!"

And so we decide to begin our third morning at the Louvre with Courbet.

"In 1918, when I arrived in Paris, I liked Ingres and Mantegna the most. Today I prefer this."

"This" is THE WAVE by Courbet.

"One feels physically drawn to it, as by an undertow. It is fatal. Even if this painting had been behind our backs, we would have felt it."

In the next room, where some insipid Chassériaus have temporarily replaced the Delacroix, among the Géricaults and Groses, his eye is soon magnetized by

the nearest of the Courbets, THE CLIFF AT ETRETAT
AFTER A STORM:

"It is fatal. With Courbet, one has the impression of
a great rock rising out of a plain. Next to it, THE RAFT
OF THE MEDUSA is beautiful, but you don't get this sense
of the force of nature."

Catching sight of THE STUDIO and THE BURIAL AT
ORNANS, he lapses into a long silence punctuated by
several volleys of "Fatal! Fatal!" He lingers before THE
STUDIO.

"The plate, or whatever it is, on the wall. You are
drawn to it. An Egyptian thing, next to that, doesn't
hold up. Magical! Those murky shadows on the left.
That brutality on the right. And Baudelaire reading:
look at that book. (It resembles a livid bird.) And the
highlight, near the temples."

Miró steps closer, steps back, puts on his glasses, takes
them off, mutters tsk! tsk! while nodding his head, without once taking his eyes off the immense canvas. People
stop, stare at him, move on.

"Incomprehensible, that indifference of theirs! And
yet there is a physical force in that painting! They are
like people who don't feel the sun beating down on
them and get burned."

We approach the BURIAL, and here I am given an in-
sight into the way, in art, things encounter, influence
each other and are linked. It is an embrace between the
eye and the object so intimate that one cannot know
which aroused the other. Thus, in this BURIAL, which I
imagined I knew by heart, suddenly my eyes, redirected
by those of my companion, see for the first time, on the
hem of the bluish-white material covering the coffin, six
or seven commas—zak!—that Miró might have signed
himself and that, in fact, he does sign, in a way:

"If you took just this, what a painting it would
make!" He adds: "It is wild, brutal, and at the same
time there is that finesse. He is one of the greatest men

*in the history of art. What a museum you would have
if you only put things with this kind of power in it.
Even all mixed up, I wouldn't care!"*

One last look at the Galerie—*"Only Gros's* BATTLE
OF EYLAU *holds up beside the Courbets"*—and on to the
Beistegui Collection. Miró pouts. *"The eighteenth century? No! Watteau? Yes!"* And yet, before Goya's
MARQUESA DE LA SOLANA he smiles, sighs: *"As simple as
a Chinese wash."* And Corot's WOMAN WITH THE PEARL
causes him to make a supplicating gesture. *"With that
pearl, ping! Ah, yes. . . . Ah, là, là."* Of the Ingres
nearby, he says: *"Very beautiful, but after you have
seen the Corot portrait . . ."*

On account of the Delacroix exhibition, the Grande
Galerie is half closed. Nothing looks familiar, not even
the MONA LISA, trapped as she now is in a dead end. I
am reminded of the guide in a Loire château who for
years had reeled off explanations learned by heart for
the benefit of tourists. One night all the works were
moved around. The next day, pointing to a Renaissance cabinet, he enjoined the visitors to admire a
Daumier. And when nobody seemed taken aback, he
continued in this fashion until the end of the tour.

Ours is not likely to last much longer, for Miró has
grown somber again and quickened the pace. In the
Italian section, he stops only before Uccello's BATTLE OF
SAN ROMANO, now flanked—a happy result of the recent
rehanging—by the two great Mantegnas: *"One comes
back to the great works. I still like Mantegna a lot, but*

it remains cold." Not until we have reached the other end of the Galerie does Miró emerge from his silence again. In front of Poussin's self-portrait: *"He is really somebody too!"* And AUTUMN, SUMMER, THE BACCHANALE WITH THE LUTE PLAYER elicit from him those little noises and gestures in which admiration and attention are mingled.

We charge through the Flemish room, the room of Medici Rubenses. By the Rembrandts we pause. I dare not confess to Miró that I am done in. He asks anxiously, *"We're not going to look at the entire Louvre, are we?"* And I tremble at the thought that, had it not been for his own fatigue, we *would* surely have seen it all, so conscientious and painstaking is my companion. We reach the exit, remarking that although we had stayed a shorter time than on our two previous visits, we were nevertheless more exhausted. (Was it the fault of what we had been looking at?) In passing, the Pietà of Avignon prompts him to comment, without my quite knowing whether it is a compliment or a criticism: *"That's something serious, that one."* At any rate, only the MARTYRDOM OF SAINT GEORGE by Martorell, a sort of Catalan Bosch, horrible in its cruelty, succeeds in restoring Miró's gay spirits.

Now, let us try to understand. And to do that, it is wise to note that everything we have said, thus far, falls into three categories. At one extreme, those short, pithy, incisive remarks that only Miró could have made. At the other extreme, but no less peculiar to Miró, the long stretches of silence. Between these two limits, finally, approximating the first in form but the second in content, an assortment of remarks that any man of taste could have made, if it were not for the fact that Miró's taste—Corot-Rembrandt—again reflects the polarity I have just indicated. And just as Miró indis-

criminately welcomes delicatesse and immensity, so the
microbe's eye and the sledge-hammer blow are intimately linked in his work and in the concept he has of
all works. He seeks out the detail but immediately
blows it up to the dimensions of a temple wall or a
public square.

This faculty for radiation or propagation is not
granted to just any detail. Those that Miró chooses are
concentrations of vital energy seized at the critical moment of its birth: at the sharp, precise point at which
the cactus, the rock break through the smooth surface of
the earth. In the same way, the unexpected detail
erupts out of the canvas, out of the accepted context of
our habits, of history. And the characteristics of this
sudden apparition are easily deduced. It gives a shock,
it wounds (are not blades all the more dangerous when
they are thinnest?), it is cruel. Like the awakening of
the newborn at his first breath. Shocks deform, the ball
we thought was round is shown, through photography,
to be flattened at the moment of impact: the misshapen,
aysmmetrical, bruised and battered forms dear to Miró
are but the consequence and proof of his pursuit of
moments and points in which a striking power asserts
itself. The CONSTELLATIONS, which occur at the highest
point in his career (I can find only one equivalent to
them: the SACRAMENTS Poussin painted for Chantelou),
are the most unearthbound version of the stars his will
to shock has never ceased provoking the sight of.

That the slightest pin prick should be felt as a
sledge-hammer blow, that the amoeba should resemble
a monstrous dinosaur is not astonishing either. Pain
and surprise are absolutes and all the more so in that
all reference points have disappeared: in the dark, any
hand that grabs you is the hand of an ogre. When the
lights go back on, the ogre becomes your brother again.
Miró does not like established orders in art, especially
if they are maintained, as in Assyria and Egypt, by

tyranny. In them, the effects of mass, even the most colossal, do not shock at all, for they are expected. And of course, his need for the unpredictable can be more easily gratified today than in those imperious epochs: time has left the thrones of the past empty, and the present has none at all. Once the languages of which they were the carriers are forgotten, the signs of the old civilizations become lines more or less beautiful, gestures, thus acquiring a sort of relationship to the non-significant gestures of contemporary painting. Miró's eye can search at leisure through the Louvre for the vivacious little part liberated from the constraint of ancient hierarchies, of old duties and convictions, and believe that, as it is everything in his work, it is also so in the works of the past; in short, that his art, in isolating in its pure state that concentration of energy, constitutes the end result of the history of painting. The fragment (torn from its context by the ravages of the centuries or by Miró's attention) on the scale of a fresco, says he, what a work of art that would be!

But the fragment (of a whole) and the detail (self-sufficient, in Miró's way) are not equivalents. The latter is absolute, pure individual creation, a fly's eye which appears to be a dragon's eye because there is no longer a basis for comparison, a scale (the scales themselves sway like mobiles in Miró's paintings). The former is relative; it is a point situated against a cultural, religious and philosophic horizon. It never erupts onto an empty canvas, but only a populated one. Its arrival obliges all the pre-existent forms to make an adjustment; in return, they force it to compromise with their presence. Even isolated, later, by some chance, the fragment will bear witness to this necessary integration, these reciprocal impacts.

We are beginning to get a glimpse of Miró's situation. The horizon, toward the end of the First World War, had disappeared, so to speak. The individual word no longer inserts itself, willy-nilly, into the general language. Until the Renaissance, the work of art had participated in the world; from the Renaissance to the twentieth century, it had imitated it—in its appearances at first, and finally, with Cubism, in its presumed structures. It had been real, then realistic. Even when a rule laid down by a priest or a despot had not explicitly imposed a message on the artist's work, a general, diffuse presence of religion or reason converted the particular gesture into a sign. Now, all that background was depopulated, left to silence.

Miró's silence has no other origin. In truth, for a scrupulously honest painter—but perhaps none is Miró's equal in this respect—there could be no answer but silence. For the artist has nothing to say: it is his civilization which holds the keys to language. He can only cry out, and hope that his interjection will be welcomed into the tightly woven verbal fabric. He is a point that only the horizon can situate.

Exclamations, remarks that are scarcely more than cries, and silence: thus, it is by its very limits that Miró's conduct, at the Louvre and in his work, seems to me to be faithful to the present and, consequently, significant. His cult of "detail" answers the strictest logic: it is what a man alone can produce without lying. Lying? Believing or pretending to believe that the context exists outside or that the painter is capable of creating it out of his own knowledge as Surrealism claimed to when, in hypostatizing the imagination, it thought to confer an objective existence on the subjective. What places Miró in the margin of Surrealism is precisely that he does not cross the frontier beyond which experience turns into mythology. His fantastic universe dies as soon as it is born: his monsters are not durable and manageable balloons, but bubbles that form above the broth of personal experience, burst and fall back into it. If we must at all costs find an exemplary scheme in Miró's protean work, it is not in one of his innumerable fairy-tale aspects that I would look, but in those canvases where one spot, one point, one sinuous or dotted line is dropped into the void.

Only artisanship can face this void without being paralyzed by fear. The sensitive hand can do without the horizon. The artisan is certainly not blind, but he keeps his eyes lowered. Then, is Miró not looking for a loophole when he proclaims his love of the artisan? His concern about the book, his penchant for illustrating texts written by poets, do these not betray a nostalgia for being the illustrator of a given word? But nostalgia is the opposite of identification. The book is incomprehensible from now on, the writing lost or undiscoverable. Far from bringing the artist closer to the artisan, the invading silence separates them, since the artist only becomes an artisan when a culture expresses itself through him.

It might be, then, that the work is fragile, slight: that does not make it minor. What was full in the past is empty today: but it is the same space, source of all graveness. At no moment has Miró turned his back on it. Dead are the gods who peopled it, but he has not sought to replace them with false gods. And thus the space finds itself full of a new meaning, the last possible meaning: the absence of all gods. Nothing comes to attenuate the confrontation of the little shock and the great silence, which cause even the comic to lead to the ample, the solemn: do we laugh at a clown's somersault when he performs it over a void? Miró has always been jumping off into the void.

If one of us throws himself into it, he loses his balance and his body falls awkwardly, ridiculously, like a disjointed puppet. Miró, however, falls so elegantly that one might think he was flying, not falling. He does not beat his arms desperately: everything is neat, precise, free—fatal. Can the detail have managed, after all, to create an order based on itself alone, the way a rock thrown at a window makes cracks radiate on the pane? Is it like a very hardy plant that can grow in a simple glass of water?

But the plant only keeps growing up to a certain point. Then, it must be rooted in soil. Miró's good fortune has been that, in the evolution of painting, his career coincides exactly with this short interval. His genius is to have known how to seize this opportunity. Like those people in cartoons who, propelled into space, continue to act for a few seconds as though they still had their feet on the ground, Joan Miró's work has marvelously been able to exploit this brief suspended moment that history has granted between meaning and silence.

Pierre Soulages

"*Truthfully,*" he mutters, "*I'm not an art lover.*"

A fine beginning. Does one have to hate the Louvre, then, to be an artist?

"*We brag about having such a beautiful museum, but there's an enormous gap: it skips from Rome to Cimabue. The Romanesque period is missing. Does that mean they didn't paint? Not to mention prehistoric art, stashed away at Saint-Germain-en-Laye. Now those are just the things that I love best.*"

I take heart again. It is not hatred, just frustrated love. He tells me—and his somber mood brightens as he talks—that his tastes have remained the same since childhood: the harsh plateaus of the Causses rather than laughing valleys, tree trunks denuded rather than in the season of swirling leaves, the engraved menhir statues at Rodez, the abbey at Conques.

"*That's what gave me the crucial shock. At the time, in school, they were lecturing us about the touching awkwardness of the capitals. But I found them over-whelming, and never stopped to wonder whether they were clumsy or artful.*"

When we got to the foot of the great staircase, and did not head for the upper floors devoted to painting, but went around them instead toward Romanized Africa, toward the Near East, Arabia, toward Sumer, it was not by chance at all, or out of a simple desire to avoid the crowds. Soulages' deep affinities are with stone, with matter. Isn't the Romanesque, above all, an architect's style, a sculptor's, a goldsmith's, an enameler's? In comparison, Romanesque painting, frescoes or illuminations seem vacillating, flimsy. In its monumental stature, its mass that sensibility cannot mold at will, but caresses, hollows, engraves, cuts into like water running over a rock, Soulages' painting resembles erect stones, steles, crowned columns, old rustic furniture.

But these physical qualities, which should have led Soulages into sculpture, are expressed through the paintbrush. His work is not stone but a "dream of stone," precisely as was the quattrocento painting we are turning our backs on. For the pictorial illusionism of the Renaissance is born of a nostalgia for space—that space to which sculpture, by its very nature, had direct access. Giotto was inspired by Roman bas-reliefs, and Uccello's horseman, in the Duomo, clearly shows how great was the painters' desire to challenge sculpture's monopoly on thickness. An insane dream, to be sure, and one that leads to anguish. But doesn't the same hold true for Soulages? Balance, of course, but unstable balance. Anxiety lurks beneath the structure's beautiful order: very like the alert eye, or rather the eye-on-the-alert, which belies, in some way, the calm assurance of the large body striding along beside me, coming to a halt before a fragment of carved rock from Sud-Oranais (El Hadj-Meimouh).

"This is moving. The cuts follow the cracks in the stone so closely that you can't tell where the carving takes over from nature. It's like the Altamira bison: the rock was already a bison before the painter got involved

*with it. It is this confusion, which is a fusion, that I
love. Between the accident of the stone and the will of
the engraver an understanding is born similar to that
which arises between the will of the modern artist and
the unknown he confronts."*

Unexpectedly, I remember my companion bending
over a copper plate bubbling in an acid bath, watching
the ravages of the biting liquid, intervening to rescue
the work from nature's accidents and bring it back to
the desired form. I think again of his need, in front of
the canvas, to abandon himself to that heedless intuition which is linked with nature, the bestower of
powers.

And yet, Soulages' painting is born of conscious
choices, of a minute study of the means, of controlled

gestures. Instinct and anxiety, design and matter: again
the contradiction—like veins through which two incompatible bloods flow, one of a stay-at-home, the other
of a wanderer—which must be resolved.

*"We don't know the why of the choices we make.
When I know why I like a thing, I already like it a little
less. A work is interesting in the degree to which it
escapes its creator's intentions and the spectator's in-
terpretations."*

"A door must be closed to be interesting. But then
we're wasting our time here. At the Louvre, the doors
open, the works speak."

*"We make them speak. We think we understand
them, but the agreement rests on a misunderstanding—*

luckily, for this misunderstanding is fertile. I believe in the fruitful misinterpretation, the productive incomprehension. When the professors tell you, 'What the painter or poet was trying to say here,' you can be sure they're about to teach you something completely useless. It's good to visit museums with artists, because they make you see in the canvases and objects what is not in them."

"So, art that resists understanding will not resist misunderstanding? You accept the idea that the doors open on the condition that they're opened with false keys."

"The works I like the best are those that correspond to an interpretation I give them while at the same time eluding it."

Here I am, once again, in the presence of a contradiction firmly imbedded in the deepest part of Soulages' personality: between design and mystery, mind and matter. And it is surely not by chance that the first object to catch his eye was this modest Sud-Oranais stone: it illustrates the troubling duality that seems to obsess him, and brings comforting evidence of a possible solution, through *fusion*. The hope that there exists a border, a point where the human scheme and the natural scheme coincide. And perhaps Soulages is an abstract painter because the abstract, as he practices it, permits simpler schemes than the figurative. It is more apt, consequently, to allow reduction to a common denominator which would abolish the rupture between man and the presence which besieges him from all sides, rises up under him, weighs upon him: the real.

"It's always a question of the real. In figurative art, it is there in the form of appearance; in non-figurative art, it is there in the form of experience. It's still thanks to the world that the painting stripped of appearance has a meaning. The real is the set of relationships we have with the world. Appearance is only one of these relationships, and one of the most superficial. Why

*should we choose precisely this one to express our rap-
port with the world?"*

Superficial, because complex: only abstract simplicity
can fit into the narrow crevices the world offers for our
penetration into her bosom. And don't we have proof
that this simplicity is fundamental when we feel a kin-
ship, despite their cultural remoteness, with so many of
the works from ancient times reposing here?

Soulages advances familiarly through the Chaldean
halls. THE ARCHITECT WITH THE RULER is not foreign in
the least to him. And while Sumerian writing was an
enigma to scholars for a long time, he recognizes it at
once as a bald gesture toward stubborn matter.

*"I like the mineral, crystalline look that cuneiform
writing on a stele acquires."*

History, like anecdote, is a superficial appearance;
understanding is easily reached beneath its skin-deep
mysteries. Standing in front of the stele of Zakir, King
of Hama (Syria), with its powerful tiers of rectangles:

*"A photo of that would remind you of my engrav-
ings! That big black form, which isn't really geometrical . . ."*

The more you encompass, the less you embrace, says
a French proverb. Inordinately comprehensive categories lose their meaning, fall into a mechanical clas-
sification. I think of minds that have improperly
digested psychoanalysis, recognizing in every form, con-
cave or convex, a sexual symbol, masculine or feminine;
the shapes of things being what they are, these people
find erotic obsession everywhere, and thereby banalize

it. But it would be misreading Soulages' anxious intelligence to suppose he had not already thought of that himself:

"It's almost too close to me."

He laughs, embarrassed, turns away, and notices a MAN'S HEAD from Hauran.

"Terrific! Actually, that head is closer to me. A form can only be a crude envelope. A face is always round, two holes for the eyes, another for the mouth, and yet there are faces and faces. One mustn't be too taken in by crude designs. That the Zakir stele resembles my engravings is true, grosso modo, *but art isn't* grosso modo.*"*

And, a few steps farther on, about a statue, he says: *"Like all things seemingly violent and simple, it all hangs on subtleties—a reflection, a slight fold."*

That is why Soulages' painting, despite its need for simple forms where natural order joins with the mind's, is not purely geometric. Orthogonal designs are the tail the lizard leaves with us so he can get away. Soulages' painting seeks to be an anxious geometry, participating in the world's chaos and in human coherence. Whence *the fascination of the almost symmetrical.* The spirit of subtlety rescues the spirit of geometry, provided it does not completely confuse its order. My companion's eye unfailingly lights on works where simplicity is qualified by subtlety, where an unstable balance holds sway. His own painting illustrates this principle, imposed on him by the double exigency of his temperament, but does it not also—and such coincidences between personal necessity and historical necessity are the artist's good fortune—illustrate the historical conjuncture which situates Soulages' emergence, right after the Liberation, at the precise moment when formal abstraction died, when action painting was about to be born? Painting which is already an action, but in which gesture still preserves the weight of form. No longer immobility, not yet agitation: slow action.

Is the principle of unstable balance, in the long run, closer to reality than that of stable balance? From an art of synthesis one slides surreptitiously into a synthetic art. The formula, unhorsed for a moment, gets back into the saddle, and the willful, fragile mind rides higher than ever. The real, which is no longer conjured save in appearance, marshals its threats. Then anxiety awakes once more. The alerted intelligence bewares its alliances too hastily concluded with the unknown. And one comes to hope for the violent eruption one had sought to prevent by provoking and channeling it. Before the WILD BEAST CHAINED TO A DISK (Mesopotamia) :

"What interests me the most here are the cracks in the mold."

Without stopping, we walk through the Assyrian galleries with their dazzling testimonials to tyranny. Then come the vestiges of the Greek and Roman presence in Asia Minor. Shafts of decapitated columns, marbles chiseled to hold forever the impression of a perfect image of man which seem, nevertheless, to have suffered mutilation more than any other art. But perhaps it is only because none has so rejected the eventuality of mortal imperfection, of ruin.

"What's always interested me in Greek statues is the way in which they break. Sometimes, the accident of the break adds something—the disclosure of the vein? Nature springs up again beneath the artist's intention. We can see the exciting clash between art and nature,

sometimes the alliance. . . . It is to the extent that I can sense through the form something that lies beyond the intention, even of style, beyond the meaning, the image, that it touches me. Catastrophe or neglectfulness are thus factors of revelation."

To accept, to welcome the break because finally through it the truth is manifested unequivocally in its pure state: raw matter. And at the same time—for it is not in the nature of the artist to desire his own death—to hope to survive the disaster. Thus is clarified my companion's taste for the arts called barbaric or regressive: they are breaks in the high civilizations.

"Negro art takes the modern conscience by storm. The Gallo-Romans besieged, bent Roman culture, as raw nature reclaims, through catastrophe, artistic perfection. And yet, the essential endures. It is that, rather than periods settled in the comfort of their skills, that touches me."

Back at the intersection near the WINGED VICTORY, I cannot help asking him if he ever goes upstairs.

"I used to go up there often, in 1946, when I first came to Paris. Before that, I'd only known the museum in Montpellier: Géricault, Courbet, Delacroix, Veronese (THE MYSTICAL MARRIAGE). *Montpellier was for me a little like Claude Lorrain's Rome. It was there that I first learned to love Poussin. I came to the Louvre to see everything I didn't know about, to fill myself in. I had a few favorites: Uccello's* THE BATTLE, *a Cranach . . . But actually, that wasn't too important to me. It was a student's curiosity, not a deep attraction."*

In truth, his essential categories had already been forged; he must have seen Western painting through them as he does now, as I drag him upstairs toward that world inaugurated by Cimabue's VIRGIN WITH ANGELS:

"What I find very beautiful in Cimabue are the re-

mains of Byzantine hieraticism, and again, at the same
time, something new being about to happen, that one
can only sense."

The large body freezes, the anxious eye darts, stares:

"*The fascination of the almost symmetrical . . .
You can take this painting apart, like a machine, and
yet its mystery remains unexplained. And that's what
troubles me, and gives it its power over me. It's a canvas which resists; and yet it seems to depend on systematic and fairly simple compositional methods. Even
in its logic, something escapes logic. That's what interests me. For in itself it is nothing, For some, such
rigor is a necessity, but only as one of the terms of the
dialogue, which is poetic. Certain poets need prosody,
but prosody is not poetry. What is always necessary is
the dialogue, for the dialogue is a contest, and contests
are productive. Here, look!*"

The example is unexpected: we are standing in front
of Fra Angelico's CORONATION OF THE VIRGIN.

"*In its order, in its harmonies, the upper part is
rather two-dimensional, decorative. In contrast, the
predelle, below, open up a space in perspective. There
are two different visions, as if in the theatre the painted
curtain were raised a little, and one could see, underneath it, the stage disappearing into the distance. And
yet, the predelle are not an accessory: they are part of
a dialogue. The depth which the predelle open up
under the painting make it seem to come forward.*"

As we talk, a guide stops near us and delivers a strictly anecdotal account of the CORONATION to his audience. And it seems to me that here is a striking case in which thematic and structural analyses, far from contradicting one another, mutually clarify each other. There truly are two visions, in effect: that of the predelle recounts historical events, that of the painting above presents divine hypostases. Below, the vanishing perspective tells of the passing of time; above, the decorative frontality proclaims the eternal present. By this duality of vision, the artist reproduces in his imagery the great Christian debate between the City of God and the City of Man opened by Saint Augustine. And in succeeding in giving it, plastically, the form of a dialogue, he is also answering a redemptory hope.

"Furthermore, here is the proof of this interdependence between the painting and the predelle," says Soulages, who has gone up to Giotto's SAINT FRANCIS. *"The whiteness of the predella in the middle is made indispensable by the two white houses on either side of the painting. And yet, it's always photographed without its predelle. When you separate the decorative devices from the significant surfaces of the painting in a work of this sort, you're surely making a mistake. They can't be separated. A living thing won't allow itself to be dissected."*

Once again, penchant for a system provokes in him the defiance of the system. Drawn to the small MARTYRDOM OF SAINT COSMO by Fra Angelico, in which five pine trees surge up above the drama, he says:

"Those five straight black flames in the middle of the painting, or almost in the middle!"

Logic, anxiety, oscillating from one to the other, fascination with order, but also with contradicted order: I can easily recognize in passing Soulages' fundamental theories—to the point of starting to talk like him. And I find them all the more to be the keys to his work now that he is no longer thinking about it. But are these paintings around us, from which he makes his selections, anything more than mirrors to him? Does he silver them over and obliterate their true meanings? Or, on the contrary, as a bell makes the glasses sensitive to the same wave lengths vibrate on a sideboard, can it be that his obsession has endowed a certain quality with a sufficiently percussive character to awake, in a strange work, its sleeping equivalent? Soulages peers at Mantegna's CALVARY:

"The qualities of the forms and space, despite the apparent realism . . . On the right, where the wicked thief's cross is, everything is abstract, silent. On the left, the Virgin's group, pathetic. This pathos, in Mantegna, touches me less. I'm especially sensitive to the verticals of the rocks, of that cross, to that whole immense verticality. The right side is tragic, the left pathetic. The Virgin weeps, the thief expresses himself though his lines. This unity, this scaling of space through forms, gives a tragic grandeur to the entire scene. Yes, it's not only a means of giving the scope of the drama, it's also the very tragedy of the canvas."

Must one be the victim of duality oneself to be able to detect what tears Mantegna between constructive severity and pathos? Looking at SAINT SEBASTIAN:

"The large archer at the bottom, the tiny, precise landscape in the distance. The clash betwen these two opposed spaces, the disturbance it creates, that's what is gripping: the confrontation between the realism of one detail and the unrealism of an immensity, violently juxtaposed. In any case, it's less overwhelming than the CALVARY. *The effect here is more intellectual than plastic. It derives a little too much from the figuration."*

On the opposite wall, Uccello's great battle, learned and barbaric, instrument of black magic that stands out among the illustrious specimens of humanism lining this part of the great gallery.

"In 1946, I used to come here just to see it. It's one

Pierre Soulages: UNTITLED PAINTING

Paolo Uccello: THE BATTLE OF SAN ROMANO

*of the most important works in the Louvre. That's be-
cause of its rigorous design: those lances, that stamping
of legs, those repetitions, that verticality perpetually
broken by diagonals, the space which the repeated
pounding creates, uniform in appearance, and the whole
lightened by a few decorative curves* [the standards].
*There is also the color, even though it is damaged: it
is independent of the light. But it's shameful to talk
about this painting so superficially. I feel as if I'm muti-
lating it."*

A silence, and then:

*"That inextricable mixture of coherence and inco-
herence . . ."*

"In the BATTLE at the Uffizi, we see the conquered
fleeing before the conquerors and, in the background,
some rabbits on the run, pursued by hunters. The
composition of the painting is arranged on two diagonals which, starting from the bottom of the picture,
meet near the top, thus forming a triangle. Now, the
conquerors, like the hunters, closely follow the line on
the right; the conquered, like the game, diverge from
the one on the left. It is as if Uccello had wanted to
tell us that deviation from geometry weakens us, that
strength lies in obeying the mathematical law whose
lines are, in the most literal sense, lines of force. Or, if
you like, that as a mast is needed to hold the sails aloft,
so an abstract armature is needed to support the figurative image."

*"On the condition that you don't limit the founda-
tion to a few primary figures, to pure geometry. One of
my favorite paintings at the time, although I started
liking it after the Uccello, was Giorgione's* THE COUNTRY
CONCERT. *The two legs and the flute used in the prolonging, the balancing of the two nude women, the
balance of the arm and the hip . . . that rigor amidst
the grace. The architecture of that painting? Oh! là là!"*

"Isn't it dangerous to attach ourselves to this extent

to the skeleton of a painting, to the detriment of its flesh? It seems to me that we're X-raying the work, not looking at it."

"You make me exaggerate. The subject counts, of course, whether one is looking at a Virgin or a cow. But what counts even more is the dialogue between the image and what it evokes without being able to state it outright, between the figurative forms and the subjacent geometry. They mutually bend each other, are necessary one to the other. Look at Veronese's THE WEDDING FEAST AT CANA. *There's the great, well-disciplined orchestra, finely tuned. The strength of the whole is not lost despite the diversity and virtuosity of its parts. We can take it in at a glance or wander through it detail by detail just as well. And the artist carries out this enterprise in unison. Look at the large square of sky; underneath it is a circle, and, at the end, Christ."*

Even though Soulages admits to the necessity of a dialogue, his sympathies lie with one of the participants, the one which, from the Renaissance to the twentieth century, has been pushed beneath the surface. In Titian's VENUS DU PARDO, he emphasizes the *"upwards, to the right!"* that one feels everywhere. And before El Greco's CHRIST: *"The two prelates, one black and white, the other white and black . . . Christ's body, which participates in the rhythm of the sky . . . One even wonders if there would be a sky . . . if there hadn't been a Christ first."* Isn't it because the surface sets a trap for us with its Circean charms: the mirages of perception?

"The great works of the Renaissance and post-Renaissance are like gear boxes: I wouldn't like to put my hand in one."

To discover the structure subjacent to the surface image is to break the spell. But to apprehend it is to prove that one is sensitive to it. Tintoretto's SUSANNA AND THE ELDERS makes him say:

"The space in this painting, fascinating! It belongs more uniquely to this painting than to all the theories of perspective. I'm enthralled."

Before the PORTRAIT OF MADAME RIVIÈRE by Ingres:

"One can't say that one is happy to see this canvas, but it does have a demented, lashing quality. It's one of the great things in painting. Heaven knows why!"

One of the goals of painting consists precisely in making the image-surface so perfect that one no longer dreams of transgressing it. While he admires such perfection, Soulages, to all appearances, is troubled by it. I notice him heave a sigh of relief when we get to THE BURIAL AT ORNANS:

"Incredible! The color, the gravity of it . . . The great horizontal . . . All the highlights on the left, and a large black mass on the right . . . The worn, flat color . . . One of the great canvases of French painting . . . The blacks . . . (he laughs, embarrassed, like someone who suddenly notices he has been pleading, without meaning to, *pro domo.*) *It's as hard as a rock, while in* THE RAFT OF THE MEDUSA *there still are some rhetorical effects."*

What he admires in Courbet is what an artist who

wants to lend to painting the substantiality inherent in sculpture must dream about. On the deserted roads of Courbet's countrysides, the stone pushes against and sometimes breaks through the eroded surface of the asphalt (*the worn, flat color*) : thus, something immense, material, mute drives through the rustic imagery. And there, along with the narrative ideal and pure painting, is a third possible goal to painting: the substantial captured by superficial art—in other words, a reconciliation between the mind and its opposite, nature. Doesn't the passion for black that possesses Soulages (it accounts to a large extent for his attachment to Delacroix's WOMEN OF ALGIERS—"*one of the paintings I have loved the most*") come from the fact that black, elevated by paintbrush and palette knife to the rank of color, isn't really a color at all? Let us say that, in their sunny assembly, it is a survivor from a very primitive reign: rather like powerful Hecate, the only Uranian divinity whom Zeus, after the triumph of the Olympians, allowed to retain her privileges, according to Hesiod. Hecate, goddess of Earth. Is she not, according to the old theogonies, the daughter of Chaos and Night, of Night which is black? Soulages, thank God, is more straightforward:

"*Black? I've always loved it, even in my childhood paintings. I preferred trees in winter, the season of wet tree trunks. It has always remained the basis of my palette. It's the most intense, the most violent absence of color, conferring an intense and violent presence to colors, even to white: as a tree makes a sky blue.*"

"A propensity for dark moods, perhaps?"

"*Not at all, there's no sentimentality in my taste for black: in China, black is not the color of mourning. Simply, I see black: at the Beaux-Arts, they made us draw a plaster cast of I don't know which ancient marble. I was seated facing the light: my discus thrower was as black as ebony.*"

"Isn't that discovering the art of the past?"

"Yes, as a navigator discovers a continent rather than as an engineer discovers the principle of a machine."

We only believe what we recognize. The art of the past exists, but only our art can discover it. For the historian, today is born of yesterday; for the creator, yesterday is born of today.

"Then what's the point of looking into the past?"

"My work is narrowly limited by the possibilities of my profession, of my times. So, when I suddenly become aware of the back of a basalt sculpture, very remote from me, from what has served me and surrounds me, I am moved and comforted."

Bram Van Velde

Is any painting more radical, more solitary than Bram Van Velde's? He says: *"I am so involved with shedding light on a personal situation that I follow in nobody's footsteps."* What language can be borrowed from others? What message brought them? *"Painting is an attempt to capture oneself. I do not know what it is to be abstract."* For according to him, at least so I suppose, to be abstract is to love, more than the figurative artist, painting for itself, love it to the point of eliminating the object to be represented, which formerly kept it from coming into full flower. Nothing of the sort with Van Velde, obsessed, to borrow the words from Samuel Beckett's last novel—he is the one who quotes him—by "the thing, always the thing, someplace," the thing that must be found, closed in on, shown. Does he lack technique, talent, as much as he claims? Surely not, but he bullies them as an anchorite castigates his body, as a learned theologian, touched by grace, willingly limits himself to telling his beads. *"I learned to paint as a house painter. Some paint in a bucket, a brush. I do not know how to draw, really. If I achieve a drawing in my painting, it is created by the color, by the thing to*

be transmitted, to see and to show." Which is none
other than himself. *"I am in a thousand pieces: painting makes me one, as it were."*

And yet, he is not involved with Expressionism any
more than with abstraction. Not confession but conversion, an operation of salvation. The work does not
suggest the image of the intolerably painful self:
through it, the self seeks the missing element that will
make its destiny bearable, if only for a moment, the
place—the expression "someplace" crops up often in

Van Velde's conversation—the miraculous place where
the thousand pieces will fit together again. *"Painting re-
builds me. That effort toward the image causes me to
see anew, and thus I can begin again."* A painting by
Van Velde looks to me like an effort to localize, through
marks as precise as those on a map, this essential self
which slips away, which he knows will never let him
rest, the search for which he can, however, never abandon. *"It really is shocking,"* he says with rage, *"that
one cannot cheat in a world where all people do is
cheat."*

The essence of Van Velde's adventure is this: he ex-
poses the Achilles' heel that others shield. *"Painting*

lives only through sinking into the unknown in one-self.'' It begins with that fault that haunts the most ac-complished masterpiece and is like the signature of the finiteness of man, its author. Van Velde let himself sink into it, knowing, accepting the weakness, the rid-icule, the impotence, the blindness it imposes on him, refusing to cling to the edges, consenting only to this plunge where he runs every risk of losing himself. To-day, he has so totally assumed this fatality that one has some trouble conceiving what is so dizzying and hor-rible about the choice—supposing that he acted out of free will—to identify only with that part of the self which is so close to nothingness. And so, I like to remember Van Velde's painting at that distant time when it had a history, and when it still fitted into the history of painting. *"At that time,"* he says, *"I thought I was capturing the real world, but many things in my painting already indicated that that was not so. For ex-ample, the violet face in the middle of the white land-scape: its expression is so empty that one cannot bear it. That was I. Every painting that has a life lives on moments like that."* A peasant working his field sees a tiny fissure open up in front of him, from which comes a thread of smoke. He goes around it, and does the same the next day but with more difficulty, for the crack has widened, and the day comes when all his land falls into the burning, bottomless crater: thus were Van Velde's landscapes, still-lifes and figure paintings subverted by a secret crack. The appearances of the real, the certain-ties of geometry were emptied of their *raison d'être*. The language learned (from Breitner, the German Ex-pressionists, the Fauves, Picasso) became less and less suited to the dark mouth that gaped in the canvases, making it clumsy, absurd. A spectral presence—or more exactly an absence—haunts them, recognizable only through its effect on the visible forms, which finally seem less real than it does.

One day, Van Velde stopped trying to cover up this breach and dedicated himself exclusively to it. Until then, artists had banked on their strength: Van Velde was the first one to deliberately put faith in his weakness. He thereby reduced painting to that vulnerable part to which Baudelaire, whom he often refers to, had brought poetry a century before. (Might not the lag be due to the fact that the arts of speech are the most pessimistic, being the only ones not based on the positive data of the senses?) From then on, for Van Velde, no help could be expected from the outside. Ordinary perception, pictorial tricks and conventions, everything which is between, sharable, transmissible—all that is no longer of any help to him, because his case is, as they say, isolated. *"I am a prisoner of my own capacity."*

He says capacity, and not incapacity. That is because, like Baudelaire, he has a deep-rooted conviction that there exists a principle of "reversibility": *"The phenomenon of painting is that someplace one can reverse the situation, that weakness becomes strength."* For him the essence of art is this conversion; it is therefore important to place oneself "in an impossible situation," since the impossible is the necessary condition of reversal. *"In the lowest depths of the prison, there is this liberty."*

But what is it, exactly? What signs shall reveal the success, no matter how precarious, to Van Velde? Here we run into the most surprising paradox. He recognizes it, experiences it whenever the obscure, intimate contest takes shape, objectifies itself, condenses into something which does not resolve the conflicts but transmutes them into presence, into a work of art. But art begins at the exact moment when the incommunicable ceases; art calls on the particular experience to make itself transmissible or to fade away. How can Van Velde, a captive of his own mad solipsism, rejecting all common vision and language, even think of such an issue?

He thinks of it all the same; indeed his work has meaning—and for him a liberating virtue—only if it is
assured, if not of the assent, at least of the participation
of a third person: *to see and show*. The profound self,
tirelessly pursued, shows itself to him only when
glimpsed by the eyes of another. Van Velde expects his
work, which he wanted to be unrelated to the art before it, to form an integral part of the vast body of
which the museum is the depositary. I ask him:

"Do you go to the Louvre often?"

"*Of course.*"

He immediately agrees to go there with me. On the
way, he tells me: "*In the past, I went because I needed
to learn.*" That went on before he became a prisoner of
his own capacity. In The Hague he had, a little earlier,
copied a head of the young Rembrandt, a portrait by
an unknown Spaniard, "*because the face fascinated
me.*" Next there was the fissure, the dizzy fall and that
absolute isolation which makes him say: "*The past,
tradition, history? I do not understand very well. They
are linked to time. But I am more involved with life,
with what is outside of time.*"

His expeditions to the Louvre did not cease for all
that, but they had other motives. "*I would go on Sun-*

days from two to five o'clock. I loved to come with that crowd. Someplace, we were feeling the same thing, a little like in the movies." The more total the solitude, the greater the desire for communion. Nowadays, his visits are less frequent. *"I no longer go out of curiosity, but from a deeper need. At times, I feel the urge. There is such a great void inside me that I must go there, as a last resort. I go involuntarily, as though feebly attracted, in a sort of vague state. I look to the left, to the right, I stop, I walk like a sleepwalker. At a certain moment, something forces me to see. It is not easy to see. It even requires a certain courage that one does not have all the time."* (Van Velde's look is absent, and then suddenly prodigiously intense, staring unblinkingly.)

At the Denon entrance, we hesitate. Right? Left? *"The Louvre is like a city, all one ever knows is one's own neighborhood."* He had never seen the mosaics from North Africa, or the Fayum portraits, toward which I direct him. They are so removed from him, he feels so uninvolved, that he becomes benevolence itself. He admires everything and, before the mosaic of the ram, declares as agreeably detached as a tourist:

"It's very beautiful."

"Beautiful?"

"Yes, but it is not my world. The world of architecture—and of works conceived for architecture—tends toward beauty. Real painting tends toward ugliness, toward panic."

Architecture is situated, like objects, in real space, where everything is simple, free from contradictions. The "decorative" arts participate in this happy state, this plenitude of things on which being has been bestowed. But Van Velde feels engaged only from the moment when painting becomes *impossible,* when its very absurdity allows it to express the absurdity of the human condition. *"From Rembrandt on,"* he says, from the invention of easel painting, from Giotto, from modern painting, we might add: from the moment painting tried to render on a thin and limited film the thickness and immensity of the existing world. Which is to say that Van Velde will recognize only *his world, his family,* on the second floor, where the whole post-Renaissance cycle is displayed. There: *"If one thinks about art seriously, it is not even serious, someplace. It is a story that is supposed to make you laugh, but makes you cry. Or vice versa."*

He bursts out laughing, and I am suddenly, acutely aware of the grotesque in the pictorial undertaking: imagine people lining up at the windows of a savings bank while the flood waters rise around them. And all the more aware in that we are going past the enormous canvases of Gros, Guérin, Girodet. David's CORONATION begins to look like a monstrous joke. But Van Velde is no longer laughing. What bothers him here is not the absurdity, but the unconsciousness of it, and I suppose that at the sight of these canvases he must feel the rage, the disgust Pascal felt for those who were enslaved by "entertainment." He falls silent, and his expression grows neutral, only really coming to life again before

Delacroix's SARDANAPALUS: *"That makes one shudder, doesn't it? It is the portrait of the voyeur. Horrible! It borders on panic, on nightmare. In my last painting, in the studio, I perceived the same stabbing. I turned it to the wall for several weeks, so as not to have to look at it. I would see this stabbing, and think vaguely of this Delacroix. But with him, the horror is in the visible; with me, in the invisible, that one can only guess at."*

Thus, Van Velde recognizes members of his family, on the level not of plastic art but of life, which for him is *"a kind of nightmare. There is something of that in every painter. Only, we have a little more courage to face it. The frontier of anguish has shifted."*

All painting is absurd, but the consciousness of absurdity, which generates anguish, strangely modifies this perspective. In the absence of consciousness, Van Velde searches in his predecessors for the secret, diffuse anxiety, without apparent motive, which is confirmed, in a sudden outburst, by the involuntary admission. Those his eyes solicit, in the museum, are the precursors, all the more convincing for being unaware of it, of his doctrine of the impossible.

Stopping before THE RAFT OF THE MEDUSA:

"That has often haunted me, with its immense element of water." He falls silent, staring fixedly, and abruptly says: *"That little sail in the distance!"* He bursts out laughing and, immediately grave again, adds: *"Horror."* The disproportion is, in truth, unbearably grotesque: that a painter who knew his craft thoroughly could have made an enormous canvas revolve around an almost invisible dot. Imagine an architect resting a pyramid on its head. And yet, it is precisely this nonsense that makes Géricault's work moving.

All during our walk, Van Velde's eye picks out the Achilles' heel, the almost imperceptible crack that makes the building wobble and lets one see, through

the breach, in the apparent coherence, a more essential truth.

Before Courbet's BURIAL AT ORNANS:

"That is earth! The faces of potato eaters. And all that black with that little bit of white. Fascinating."

I remember, for my part, that that same painting one day made me understand the incredible miracle of the "coincidence" between art and life, facture and facts: the priests' scarlet toques are demanded by the logic of the ceremony, but also, at that precise spot, by the painting which, without that red focus, would be swept away in the direction of its insistent horizontals. A marvelous conciliation. Van Velde, on the contrary, watches for the rupture, the quirk, the sign of maladjustment: the ridiculous hat on Cranach's nude Venus (is she aware of her state?), the fire glowing in the background of the Fontainebleau School painting representing, in the serene foreground, Gabrielle d'Estrées and her sister (one feels like sounding the alarm). Mindful of the crack where the collapse begins, but also a more deeply meaningful impossibility, a saving flaw in the making. Flaws . . . Van Velde's attraction for the obsessional, for the mania that transforms the most intolerably assured person into a victim, becomes clear.

A few seconds ago, he was describing Sardanapalus as a voyeur. Then before a Tintoretto, which he is unaware is a self-portrait, he says:

"That must be of himself. It is so expressive, strange, deep. A fascinating look. One does not see it, but one feels it. So spiritual."

He thinks, and during that time the canvas is inundated by that look, as if my companion's remark had caused a leak in the face's fabric.

"There was talk about a love for a little girl." (Pause.) *"I seem to recall that one of those great painters really was a little monster. Watteau?"*

Beyond any doubt, this belief in the virtue of vice is the basis of his love for Brouwer. He drags me over to a scene of a smoke-filled room:

"These types stranded somewhere, victims of their passion. One can only laugh. Beaten, beaten! In those days, smoking was forbidden."

Fruitful downfall, tranquil acceptance of the intrusion of another world that removes the safety props from this one: all this is found supremely in Rembrandt. But so great is the place Van Velde gives him in his universe—he dates painting, let us recall, *from Rembrandt on*—that he will say little about him.

Before THE PILGRIMS FROM EMMAÜS:

"The unreal world passes into the real. It comes over you slowly. It is the opposite of a spectacular thing." (Long silence.) *"Moving, very close to tears."* Later, before SAINT MATTHEW, he notes *"the anguish of the hands."* The apparition with the childlike face makes him speak about his son. And finally: *"He is the first one to have painted so much mystery in life."*

Often, the quirk consists of an almost imperceptible inappropriateness of the pictorial manner to the represented fact, as in THE RAFT OF THE MEDUSA, and some-

times of a no less laughable excess of calculation, of
regularity. About the ray of sunshine that falls, straight
as a plumb line, into Claude Lorrain's swelling sea: *"It
looks like it was right in the center!"* Laugh: does it
not really look as if the artist were acting here like a
surveyor working his instruments in the middle of an
earthquake? What ridiculous pretension, practicing his
profession under such conditions:

*"The profession? Frans Hals can paint well, Rem-
brandt already less well, Van Gogh paints badly. And
yet . . ."*

And yet, one must not think that Van Velde despises

savoir-faire. When, impressed by his hallucinated interpretation of SARDANAPALUS, I in turn called his attention to the ghostly appearance of the arm in LIBERTY
OF THE BARRICADES, seeing in it the sign of the abstraction of the allegorical figure, I elicited this extremely
dry retort:

"It allows him to get to the top of the canvas."

Naturally, he says: *"I prefer those whose painting is
linked to my own history."* But whenever this history
leaves him a little peace, he knows how to appreciate

Bram Van Velde: COMPOSITION 1970

Rembrandt van Rijn: THE PILGRIMS FROM EMMAÜS

beautiful workmanship. He rejoices ahead of time in the pleasure Hobbema's THE WATER MILL will give him, finds the hand in THE WOMAN WITH THE PEARL by Corot *"adorable,"* steps over the cordon temporarily forbidding access to the alcove where Goya's LA MARQUESA DE LA SOLANA reigns: *"It is color become life."* Before a Van Dyck: *"What refinement! Almost too much for a Dutchman. One really wants to know who those two are"* (the Duke of Bavaria and the Duke of Cumberland). And he even has a kind word for Le Brun's CHANCELLOR SÉGUIER.

But one must not be astonished by these evidences of taste in an artist so little preoccupied with it. Without a boat, no shipwreck: there must be talent, in the beginning, to make the failure significant. Failure? That is reckoning without its reversibility. Somewhere, at the bottom of the abyss, the faculty of expression reassembles itself. *"I come to the museum to recognize in others the anguish which lies at the bottom of painting."* To recognize: daughter of the insoluble paradox, anguish arouses the gift that will make it not comprehensible, but visible. *"Most often, we look mechanically, we perceive a dead world. The museum gives us moments in which we see."* Painting wakes us, it is at once the shock and the remedy: *"A surface that catches my eye, that forces me to see it."* It shows me the absurdity of painting, but in such a way that it ceases to be a question I cannot answer and becomes a presence, an end in itself. (*"I accept it the way it is"*) or, as Van Velde also says, *"a thing."* A thing resembling no other, which only its own name fits. Before STAGS FIGHTING, which he discusses with me before we get to it: *"Courbet is one of those men who have made a name become a thing."* And reciprocally, a thing—"the thing someplace," the abyss common to all men—has taken the names of a few who have plunged open-eyed into it. The name of Géricault: *"Death is present in an incredible fashion"*

(PORTRAIT OF AN ARTIST). The name of El Greco: *"There is something there that one could see even without the figure. The background is so expressive that the rest is almost no longer necessary."* Thanks to them, we are a little less the victims of some nameless disaster. Absolute distress, the black constant beneath the varied episodes of human history, which certain individuals sometimes sink into and, like transformers,

change to clarity: "lamp-bearing anguish," in Mallarmé's admirable phrase. Solitary beacons in the void of time, but it is always the same light drawn up from the same night:

"Like long echoes answering from afar
In a dark and profound unity."

Their brilliant garland lights the dark channel, the adventurous path where man, at his deepest moment of deprivation, reverses the sign of his destiny. *"I notice each time with a certain astonishment that the effort to capture oneself finds a place in the development of painting."* Nothing is more easily shared than the essential solitude. In its coherence, its continuity where confusion should reign, the museum highlights the strength of this chain of recognizable solipsisms. Is it so astonishing that Van Velde should see himself as adding a new link to it?

"I was living on Boulevard de la Gare. One day a painting came to me, a fairly long thing, with an element—how can I describe it?—that defined my almost indefinable state. That thing done, I felt satisfied for several weeks. When I went out, it stayed inside me, someplace. I went to the Louvre. Then there was a moment, it was like a waking dream, in which I saw my painting all alone in a room."

At the Louvre, because *"there is no radical difference between the painting of yesterday and my own, because painting does not change in its essential approach: it is always a surface to be covered in such an intense manner that one believes in it."*

At the Louvre, but all alone:

"When one sees a painting, it is always alone."

Saul Steinberg

I was preparing to face, not without feelings of guilt, the usual objections: "I am an artist, you know. Talk isn't my forte. Besides, what can you say about it? Like mystic experience, aesthetic experience cannot be explained. . . ." In no time, Steinberg reassures me:

"I am wary of people who remain dazzled, exalted, silent in front of a painting. They believe in miracles. But it is we who must make our paradises. The true mystics have always been talkative. To honor a picture, you must tell it to yourself with every possible detail. When you freeze up, you know that you are standing before a boss."

Silence is the consequence of fear, and Steinberg hates tyranny.

"Art is a sphinx. The beauty of the sphinx is that you yourself must do the interpreting. When you have found an interpretation, you are already cured. The mistake people make is to believe that the sphinx can give only one answer. Actually, it gives hundreds of answers, or maybe none at all. Interpretation probably does not give us the truth, but the act of interpretation saves us."

The word brings salvation. And, no doubt, it is to the essential role of the word that we may attribute Steinberg's avocation:

"I am a writer. I draw because the essence of a good piece of writing is precision. Drawing is a precise mode of expression."

Indeed, caricature is not a purely visual medium but rather the most visual form that thought, language, are capable of assuming. What distinguishes the draftsman-

ship of Goya from that of Daumier is function rather
than talent. One looks at Goya; one reads Daumier.
The taunt of literature does not frighten Steinberg.

*"In art everything has a literary origin—except Ab-
stract Expressionism, which pretended to grow out of
the activity of the body, not out of thought. However,
even action painting is the intelligence of the body.
Anything that implies some sort of intelligence, of
whatever kind, belongs at least partly to the realm of
literature. The body's intelligence is the metaphysics
of the nose."*

Besides, all things speak.

*"Everything has a message: even the smell of muse-
ums. In Europe, museums smell of town halls and grade
schools; in America they smell like banks."*

If in most cases we do not perceive these messages, it
is because their richness is drowned out by a thunder-
ous vacuousness, as the noise of traffic drowns conversation in sidewalk cafés.

*"We spend almost our whole lives reading boisterous,
ready-made messages (the mail, the newspapers, traffic
lights). To decipher the other kind of messages requires an effort which we prefer to avoid making. Yet
it is this effort that renders life rich, gay and, so to say,
inexhaustible."*

Therefore, people must be encouraged to decipher
these deeper messages. But how? Laziness, sloth, routine, impel them to read only the language that is
familiar to them. One must use tricks. Let them proceed
along the track, but tamper with the switches.

"One must build attractive traps."

Steinberg's drawings are like traffic lights signaling
"You may cross now" on all sides at once: you confidently step off the curb—and are run over.

*"Humor is a very good trap. Laughter disarms and
opens the way for instinct. It is like hiccups, yawns.
When you try to repress a yawn, it comes out of your*

ears. Yawning is animal criticism—dogs yawn. Laugh-
ter is mental or maybe mineral. Let's drop this subject.
Trying to define humor is one of the definitions of
humor."

This is particularly true when Steinberg manipulates
the language used in the definition. The language is
the same, all right, but it has been placed in a different
context. Caricature, as practiced by most humorists,
fits the definition implicit in its etymology: it is loaded.
As practiced by Steinberg, caricature *unloads;* it frees
language from its customary obligations. Its burden removed, language flies out the window and into the
world of things. All that is needed is to mix up the
established circuits between sign and sense. This man,
whose drawings so often seek to upset communication,
confesses:

"Without wanting to, I have become a moralist."

At first sight, he has the modest and just a trifle
doctoral air of a chemistry professor: yet there is something disquieting in the eyes, the smile, the cap. But
after all, the chemistry professor might be on holiday
in Europe. Such is obviously the opinion of the four
schoolgirls who come to us as we are chatting in a room
filled with Roman sculpture. At once, we are plunged
into a typically Steinbergian predicament: faced with
sounds that possess the obvious earmarks of language
yet are impossible to understand. They are speaking
Spanish. Little by little, we manage to reconstruct the
question that they are absolutely convinced my companion will answer. Why are the eye sockets in the
colossal head of Antinoüs, Emperor Hadrian's favorite
page, empty? Without hesitation, Steinberg explains
that the eyes had been made of precious stones and that
when the barbarians came. . . . There follows a gesture of legerdemain so precise and so swift that one
would swear this innocent-looking gentleman had
learned the pickpocket trade in the Trastevere.

*   *   *

We begin our visit to the Louvre with the Roman mosaics. THE BATTLE OF THE AMAZONS, found at Daphne, near Antioch, dates from the third or fourth century A.D. Steinberg points to the central part, which is lost and has been filled in with cement:

"This empty space in the middle transforms the whole work into a geographical business. One can see how abstract art derives from the museum. It is there that one sees vertical floors. These gaps—how restful. That is why there are dull pages in all good novels. After this gap, the head of the dying soldiers is much more moving: like an action taking place behind a bush. It is interesting to show only a little part of things: female eroticism. . . ."

He turns his glance to the horsemen on the left:

"How elegant these warriors are! In them, the artist is the passive instrument of a period style, of decadence, rococo. . . . But when he got to the horse's teeth, the resemblance between the marble cubes and the teeth made him into a dentist making a denture for a horse. Here the mosaic became a collage and a pun. The artist also realized that the whole mosaic was made of horses' teeth. Look: everything is abstract, derivative—the horse's nostrils, for instance—except those teeth. They are real teeth."

And now it looks as if some monstrous Pegasus had spat out, by the millions, the little cubes that compose the pavement on which we tread.

"Those horse's teeth, they are everywhere. . . . Once you see something, you can no longer get rid of it, you are contaminated, you see it everywhere. Right now you, I, everything is made of horses' teeth. Of course, it is my eye that is contaminated."

And this contamination is hailed as a symptom of life: by its contagiousness the microbe proves itself alive.

A bit later, in front of a mediocre Roman high-relief:

"I am very fond of high-reliefs. They lead to such absurdities! To make the sculpture from a rock, which already is a sculpture! It is absurd, amusing, moving. Sculptors are primarily idol makers. To translate flesh into stone, for instance, is to deify man. For a stone to be admitted into the temple—the museum—it has to have been translated into bronze. Bronze is the sublimation of stone, wood is the sublimation of iron, and so on. That, by the way, is the secret of pop art."

What fascinates Steinberg in Wayne Thiebaud's pop paintings, as in the horses' teeth of the Roman mosaic, is the coincidence, perfect to the point of coalescence, of "nature" and "art" by way of a simple, basic form. Here, the cube; there, the cuisine of creamy pigment. We can no longer tell whether the artist has caught nature or whether nature has caught up with him. Later, in front of Sellajo's SAINT JEROME PENITENT:

"Marvelous! See how the trees are trimmed. Architecture first imitated trees, then the trees imitated architecture. Campaniles and minarets were invented by cypress trees."

The theme of a large number of Steinberg's own drawings is the unforeseen, upsetting, comic abolition of the distance between the artist and the world: the person drawing a table turns, without knowing it, into part of the table itself. The instrument of this trespass is the virulence of line, its ability to proliferate. Line is the common bond between man and things; the modulations of line constitute a language. And here it is necessary to take the word "literally" literally: the identity of human language and the language of things occurs at the level of the alphabet. The combination of letters draws them away from their origin and reality, turns them into envelopes of purely human sounds, into vehicles of abstract meanings. They no longer designate the world, they signify what the tyranny of man wishes them to signify. All's well, the words of a friend's letter tell you; but if you have the slightest knowledge of, or feeling for, graphology, you can easily detect the anxiety that lies behind his optimistic affirmations. Steinberg says:

"For me, seeing a work of art is, to some extent, a matter of graphology."

The man who hates all forms of despotism will seek to free the alphabet from its master, to deliver it from its semantic chains and turn it loose again in nature. When man and nature are analogous and continuous, writing means what it says. Writing is simply script: not so much signs as signatures (Steinberg's passion for signatures is well known), not an object of cognition but rather of recognition. The world is one—if we decipher the correspondences of which its unity is woven. It is a task that requires punctilious, almost paranoiac attention. Such an attitude of mind characterized the late Middle Ages and the early Renaissance, which saw the universe as a body tattooed with messages whose hermeticism was precisely the clue to their presence and to their importance.

"Herbs communicate with the curious physician through their signature," wrote Crollius in his *Treatise on Signatures,* "thereby revealing to him their inner virtues, hidden under nature's veil of silence."

There's something that doesn't quite fit in with the appearance of a chemistry professor: perhaps more like a professor of alchemy.

More numerous than Deucalion's teeth, the little cubes of the Louvre. . . . We stand before the PHOENIX, that great stone rug brought back from Tunisia:

"Amazing! Upside down, the goats' heads turn into coat hangers. And those wings, they are there to finish off the goat. That is what those wings are for, those pun butterflies. A flourish of the pen, a script. These goats with their horns and wings are the fathers of topographic ornaments."

The word "script" is uttered seemingly at random, or like a tic. Yet it is the right word. For when a goat's head becomes a coat hanger, when eagle's wings suddenly readjust themselves into giant butterflies, our attention is attracted—as long as we do not perceive exclusively either one or the other of the two terms—to the common form, to the line that binds them. The visual pun is the moment of levitation between two equally loaded messages, the moment when script, usually hidden by meanings, is unburdened, freed from the gravitational pull of significant sound, and stands for itself.

"The phoenix looks rather like a duck in a phoenix outfit—like Shriners dressed as Turks. You can see how the children of the house, on traversing this room, invented and rigorously followed the tradition of jumping over the goats, setting one foot on the rock and another on the duck."

We enter the Room of Augustus, certainly one of the ugliest in the Louvre.

"This, for me, is the real museum. At once you feel yourself surrounded by thousands of butterflies. The ceiling, the frescoes, the gilt reliefs, the marble pavement, the busts—everything clamors to be looked at. It's too much. All those butterflies staring at us."

Indeed, nothing is more dead, more hypnotic than a butterfly pinned to the bottom of a box—unless it is a perfect glass imitation of a butterfly. Steinberg contemplates the ceiling, covered with a hideous fresco in the distinguished manner of Puvis de Chavannes.

"To get rid of those too noble things that he painted on the walls of public buildings, Puvis did grotesque erotic drawings at home."

The ceiling of the next room is no less conspicuous.

"A nightmare! It is an octagon, which is a very tiring shape. And it is filled to the brim! It is the nineteenth century saying: 'Me too!' It competes with the works on exhibit, like Frank Lloyd Wright's Guggenheim."

"What in *your* opinion is the best solution for a museum?"

"There is no solution. A good museum is a dead museum."

Fayum portraits, imperial busts. . . . In front of that representing Annius Verus, who died in 169:

"The broken nose, the missing nose makes the beauty of the sphinx. Death takes the noses. A fleshy nose is a sign of life. The death's head, that is the secret of Greta Garbo's fascination. It is also Brigitte Bardot's: a gay death's head, with a baby's mouth, sensual fish lips."

Further on, a Fayum portrait, crude, beautiful:

"It is never possible to imitate primitives. You can imitate geniuses, discoverers, inventors. You can explore what they discovered—Cézanne, for instance. But a primitive is the pinnacle of a pyramid. After him, there is nothing. Rousseau, for example. . . . No offense meant, but who are the primitives today?"

Bust of a young woman, in marble:

"A real baby, with the real, suction-cup little mouth that babies have. It's the portrait of a Marine, the baby-faced killer. The face is broad as a pizza and the mouth tiny. Small-scale sensuality is what horrifies."

We walk toward the grand staircase. At its foot, a colossal head, that of Lucilla, Lucius Verus' wife:

"That enormous thing, it's bibelot. Its scale doesn't fit it. Out-of-scaleness is the symbol of tyranny. Slaves created the fussy arts of Indochina (microphilia) and bank architecture (macrophilia). Actually both are forms of necrophilia."

Lucilla, or an introduction to dictatorship: we have reached the first floor and are running the gauntlet of the mammoth Salon canvases. David to the right, David to the left. . . .

"He didn't have faith. The monster. The people of David's sort are sculptor-architects. They regard painting as a form of polychrome sculpture. They translate, transpose. The contrast of the robes in THE LICTORS *is borrowed from the engraver's grisaille. The blue is the*

stencil blue one finds in popular prints. How proud he
was of his high-relief whites!"

At THE CORONATION OF NAPOLEON:

"What an incredible thing to do! Those huge candle-
sticks, for example, painted again and again in per-
spective, what a nightmare! It is the opposite of paint-
ing, it is physical labor. Only in sculpture are art and
work connected. The sculptor needs to exercise his body.
I distrust skinny sculptors."

Fatigue is death's fifth column, sneaked into life by
dictatorship. Death sticks to David. In front of the THE
PORTRAIT OF MADAME RÉCAMIER:

"It's funereal. He has rediscovered, perhaps uncon-
sciously, the attitude of the deceased on Etruscan
tombs."

Deeper and deeper into fatigue's kingdom. Ingres's
THE APOTHEOSIS OF HOMER:

"Professor's art. Homework! How could such a mar-
velous artist fall in this trap! You can see how he tired
himself painting it. Dante changed into a caryatid by
the ram's horns of the column behind him—that's the
pedant's pun."

About Picot's LOVE AND PSYCHE:

"Classical painters, educated by statues, endow their
male figures with undersized phalluses, and this causes
confusion in girls educated by museums. The academic
artist starts to copy plaster folds from childhood. They
will remain his great love. Trees, clouds, faces—he
would like to translate everything into colored plaster
folds. Folds fascinate, they are the sensuality of children.
Van Gogh was obsessed by the ear because it contained
all folds: sheets, a woman's shape. It was a form of
eroticism. Folds tell everything—too much, in fact. One
of the painter's great worries is to make sure that no
involuntary symbols hide in his folds. Then, too, folds
are connected with the oldest of all the arts: embalming.
Folds embalm reality and thereby deify or sublimate it.

*The best folds I have seen are in a portrait of Lenin.
The draped chairs in it are the clouds in the apotheoses
—those levitations and ascensions—in the Virgins by
Raphael or Rubens. The history of art as viewed by
the historians is an embalming concern. One likes relics,
not living people. The living disturb. Churches like
administrators, not martyrs. Any museum is essentially
a wax museum."*

Fortunately, THE DEATH OF SARDANAPALUS cheers us
up.

Dictatorship, terror, fatigue, silence, or (it amounts
to the same thing) imposed speech make up the constel-
lation whose evil influence manifests itself by the disappearance of script.

*"All good pictures are based on a script, a handwrit-
ing. It we don't see this signature, this handwriting, we
enter into something frightening (with Puvis's or
Ingres's* THE APOTHEOSIS OF HOMER) *, in which it's no
longer the artist but society that paints."*

We stand before Giotto's SAINT FRANCIS RECEIVING
THE STIGMATA:

*"To represent the house, the tree, is a little like writ-
ing 'tree,' 'house.' It's like executing beautiful hiero-
glyphs. What renders pictures like* THE APOTHEOSIS OF
HOMER *frightening is the fact that their creators have
been eliminated: there is no longer any writing in them,
only a projection of images, of clichés. Whereas in the*
SARDANAPALUS, *you can always see the personal writing."*

Still, since there is a message in Ingres, there must
also be some writing. . . .

"Put it this way then," Steinberg explains, *"Delacroix's work is handwriting, Ingres's is typography."*

"Is the hand that essential?"

*"Yes. There is no writing without the hand and
everything that lies behind the hand, all the architecture that weighs on it, moves it—biology, geology, man's*

history. Writing is the tip of an enormous inverted pyramid."

"So all writing is automatically good?"

"No, there are bad kinds. In bad writing, you see society's pathological side—like those calligraphic devices they teach girls in finishing schools. Bad writing is artistic bureaucracy—it's an offense against nature. If man expresses himself only through society's means, he has wasted his life; and that is what society wants him to do."

Saint Francis, in brown serge, is kneeling at the foot of the mountain:

"Triangles, circles, rectangles: the composition (a pentagon) is very rigid but not visible. It is a tightrope-walking act. The rays emanating from the saint's hands sustain the angel's heavy image in the air. It is like a very solid mechanical toy. It is a miracle in which all the ingredients are visible. That is the beauty of miracles: they are normal, natural. The transmission of stigmata through gearshifting or geometry delighted the art historian who saw it as the invention of didactic composition."

Is it not madness to hope that an abstract, arbitrary construction such as the alphabet will correspond to the make-up of reality? However, is the distance between a picture painted around 1450 and someone who looks at it today not just as great? And yet, it would seem as if Uccello's BATTLE is the visual concretization of Steinberg's most personal preoccupations.

"Magnificent! It is a philosophic conception of painting. The most interesting thing is the monster formed by the three figures, one behind the other, on the left. The center part is the least interesting [it shows the victorious *condottiere*]. *It is writing on orders, dictated. There must always be a feebler part.*

"The only clear elements in the Uccello are the condottiere, *the heads and the rumps of the horses.*

Saul Steinberg: LOUSE POINT

Giotto di Bondone: SAINT FRANCIS RECEIVING THE STIGMATA

Everywhere else there are monsters, still-lifes. Those flags, those plumes. . . . People have tried to imitate this picture to show war's horrors. But Uccello was frightened, fascinated, by the horror of armor, of hooves. It was his nature. This metaphor of terror holds only for him. Extended to others, generalized, it becomes an allegory, hypocrisy. Strangely, the only bare thing in this picture is the condottiere's *face—because he is shown frontally rather than in profile. A profile is already a mechanism, a mask. Everything else in the painting is masked, even the soldiers' legs, which are masked by those vivid colors. These are no longer feet, toes, as in the Giotto. And the breastplates, the caparisoned horses: everything here is a masquerade. Uccello is a master of camouflage. The ground, the horizon, are masked by blackness, as well as by the cage formed by the spears. The entire scene takes place in a void. It is a battle between crocodiles, tortoises and crabs locked in a cage. On the ground, only a few tufts of the old nature remain. By losing their green color (which was suppressed by the painter himself, or by time?), these tufts of grass are bones and beards—relics in a battlefield. And the flag! A flag is always a collage, a mask. But here the flag is even more masked by its undulation, which turns it into a truly indecipherable piece of writing. But what attracts me above all is the left-hand corner: every figure wears a mask. The result is an incredible tricephalous monster.*

"It reminds me of something I saw when I was living in Santo Domingo, in *1941*. One night I woke up in terror. I sensed that there was something horrible near me. I switched on the light and saw ants, by the thousands, transporting a fat cockroach up the wall. The swarming mass was constantly changing shape—but the centerpiece and the logic of labor gave it the sinister symmetry of the coat of arms, the accumulation of visas in my passport, the political demonstrations seen from a balcony. Grouping makes monsters."

A little farther along, Perugino's VIRGIN AND CHILD
BETWEEN SAINT CATHERINE AND SAINT JOHN THE BAPTIST:
*"How marvelous! That deep green and that red! I
like it because of the oleographs I used to see as a child.
They lent exactly the same qualities to colors. It is something one likes not as painting but almost as pastry. One
looks at it with one's tongue, not with the eyes. It is
angelically simple, perfectly natural. Like Braque. However, monsters have always interested us more than
angels."*

This cult of the monstrous derives for Steinberg's
view of monstrosity as nature's revenge on the tyranny
of the noble, the conventional, the mediocre. We are
walking toward the exit when Steinberg stops short in
front of Gérard's MADAME VISCONTI. White flesh, a dress
whiter yet, stand out against the greens, blues and dark
grays of garden and sky:
*"From a distance it is a magnificent sight, this banana
springing out of the shade. All the clichés of art are
there. I would love to own something like that. A civilization which slowly created this as its image of what the*

work of art should be! It contains all the battles between Saint George and the dragon, all the Madonnas, as well as quotations from Zurbarán, Velásquez, the Venetians. . . . The background is by a great theatre specialist. In the sky, on the other hand, he has used the watercolor technique. And in the landscape, the technique of tapestry. Top and bottom have the same intensity. That man invented the photographer's backdrop. He has a special brushstroke for grass, and he has gold following exactly the meanders of the dress. . . . It's horrible. But this is a picture of Uccello's monster—or Melville's Moby Dick, the white whale."

Monstrosity is the absence of writing. But for us to be saved, it is not enough that the writing appear; it must also persist. Yet writing disappears in the process of reading; it dissolves into the meanings that have used it as their vehicle. It must therefore exist as writing, but as indecipherable writing (or as writing that no interpretation will exhaust), like those handwritten messages with which Steinberg fills page upon page. All writing finds its fulfillment in illegibility: such is the law he proclaims. There must be a good deal of truth in it if I am to judge by the difficulties (even greater than usual, no doubt because I was contaminated) which I experienced in decoding the pad on which I noted Steinberg's remarks at the Louvre.

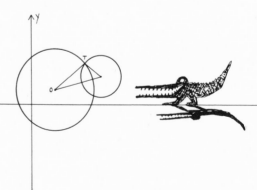

Jean-Paul Riopelle

Everything that, with the perspective of time, reveals itself to be a new link in the chain, at first strikes us—a common experience—as being a break. Even so, the work undertaken around 1947 by Riopelle and a few others seemed like a radical break with the past, even the recent past. Lyrical, or non-geometric abstraction, tachism, action or concrete painting (such were the sobriquets of the new trend) abolished the image. The image had been, until then, the common denominator of all painting, the substratum where, so it seemed, the most divergent tendencies came together and took root, the condition and mode of the transmissible in art (vision, meaning, technique) —in short, the very vehicle of the tradition. By destroying the image, painting scuttled its memory, that memory of which the Louvre is the incarnation.

A machine, installed a few weeks earlier in the vestibule, upon the insertion of a coin dispenses an admission ticket and returns the correct change. I place one franc in the slot and receive in return one ticket and fifty centimes. To Riopelle, who has done exactly the same thing, the machine returns twenty centimes.

"Some might say the gods of this temple are making you pay for having flouted them. Let's hope the WINGED VICTORY doesn't turn into the Angel Gabriel and bar our way. . . ."

But we climb the stairs without mishap.

"Did everything we see here still have meaning for you after the great break? Did you come back to the Louvre?"

"Often."

"Why?"

"It was heated. Unfortunately, they only heated the room of English painting."

Riopelle does not like interrogations at all, but today I am determined to brave a barrage of his most heavy-handed jokes and nimblest evasions. For the sake of peace, he finally says:

"I did not feel like a stranger here, afterwards. I find Lorenzetti as great as the contemporary pictures I like. I do not see the slightest difference between the past and the present. The works of the past are neither farther away nor closer to us. There has been no evolution: what has happened should simply allow us to see them better. It is so hard to see! In the old days, when I looked at reproductions of Matisse's paintings, I was convinced that they were flat. It was only much later that I realized that they had depth. That's how it is with most people, furthermore: they do not see. One day, at the Galerie Charpentier, I saw a Corot hanging upside down: the panoramic view of a landscape in Italy had become a rock. From the point of view of the subject matter, it could just as well have been a rock, but as a painting, it no longer held up, it was unbalanced. And yet, people say that a figurative painting becomes abstract when you turn it on end."

Don't they claim that it was precisely the fact of chancing to notice one of his paintings turned upside-down that put Kandinsky on the road to abstraction? In any case, the anecdote perfectly illustrates the hybrid character of his improvisations: they do not constitute a revolution, but a turning upside-down. Kandinsky inverts the image, he does not abolish it. It is quite mistaken to have tried to see him the precursor of a movement whose most noteworthy representatives are distinguished by the radical rejection of everything that had been taken for granted.

"The break was sudden, brutal, total, wasn't it?"

Riopelle slouches along, pulls his head in between his shoulders, ill at ease, annoyed.

"All the same, it came from way back. I had served my apprenticeship, drawn from nature like a maniac. But things were getting worse and worse. The last painting I did like that I worked on for two years without ever being able to finish. I didn't understand what was happening to me. I did not know that, today, the guy who wants to draw a fish on a table will not succeed."

"But why not?"

"Because there is a loss of interest. I ask nothing better than to believe in his fish—what is more formidable than one of Courbet's trout?—but he cannot make me believe in it. There was a time when the rapport between the painter and the image was alive; then it was less so; it no longer was for me at all, in 1946."

The denial of the image was not a work of destruction for Riopelle, but a certificate of the death (or of the putting to sleep) of a rapport that had been alive for a long time between the painter and the to-be-painted, the difficult return-to-the-present of an art that had let itself be invaded by the past. And I am not at all surprised, personally, that Riopelle should have played a decisive role in the perilous rejuvenation painting then underwent. I know no one, in fact, who reacts more keenly and painfully to the slightest deviation from that burning point, the instant. Painting is happiness, in the degree to which it allows one, in the span

of a work, to rejoin the present. *"To paint?"* he says. *"To put oneself in the best conditions for overflowing."* When he does not succeed in hauling himself up to the level of the present, Riopelle lags behind miserably, more deprived than anyone, positively incapable of defending himself. *"I have never hesitated at the moment of making a painting. If there is hesitation, I do not make it."* He is destined, doomed to tolerate in himself, and even in others, nothing but the present. To make a work is to recognize it in oneself. To see is to recognize it in someone else.

"In Canada, I used to go to the museum a lot. It was full of fakes and bad art. I didn't care. I went to look at a horse in the snow—calendar art, what! In 1940, the museums of Europe sent us their valuable paintings for safekeeping. I was eighteen. I went to see them hundreds of times. The last room was filled with Van Goghs. They were the first I had even seen. At the time, I liked El Greco, Tintoretto and, less, Rembrandt and Delacroix. What interested me was their technique.

They had such a lot! I would even think an academic portrait was just as great, because of its technique. Later, I realized that there was something more to Velásquez, beyond that."

"Technique, does it still have any meaning nowadays?"

"Not the same. In the old days, technique was learned by copying the masters. Today, it is the capacity to be conscious of one's own powers. A Cubist master came to see the first show I was in, on Rue Gay-Lussac. When he saw my picture, he said: 'That is not painting!' Why? Because, for him, a painter was someone who had spent six years in classes learning how to make an ear. As to the quality, the life of that ear, that did not seem to concern him. And today, all those types who used to make ears are making spots. Tomorrow . . ."

"The new technique, in short, is the awareness of what one cannot learn?"

"Yes. With experience or free intuition, one can sense when the painter is not cheating himself."

Cheating is continuing to paint when one should stop, stop because one is no longer painting in the present, because the rapport between the artist and the object which provokes the creation is no longer vibrant, but lax.

"The portrait of Rembrandt's son is a great work because there was contact between the painter and his model. Rembrandt placed his technique at the service of something else, which overflowed him . . . and also overflowed his model."

"What?"

Riopelle shrugs his shoulders, falls silent, walks on.

His rejection of the past, then, has not made him insensitive to the works in the museum, for only what was passé at the moment of its creation is ever passé: the present, once brought to life at any period, is alive forever. Riopelle recognizes it more confidently, having one day seen it emerge in himself, and pays attention only to it.

He stresses his preferences with a brief *"Superb!"*; a simple scowl signals his antipathies. Among the former: THE BUST OF MADAME DE FONTRÉAL by Carpeaux *("It's so ambiguous!")*, Da Vinci's SAINT ANNE, Uccello's BATTLE, THE VIRGIN by Veronese *("That light remains possible")*, Tintoretto's SELF-PORTRAIT *("It's an interrogation, it fills as much space as all the big works around it")*, Van Ruisdael, Potter, Watteau, Guardi *("Fabulous!")* THE DAUPHIN CHARLES by the Master of Moulins. On the subject of his dislikes: THE RAPE OF THE SABINES by David *("Nothing much is happening in the background. Everything is in the foreground. He has merely plugged the holes. In the* Petit Larousse, *Canadian edition, the only photograph showing naked breasts was one of this painting; one must conclude that David's nudities are not very dangerous")*, Ingres' Raphaelesque Virgin *("Isn't he the one who signs himself Foujita?")*, SAINT STEPHEN by Carpaccio *("Artificial light")*, Philippe de Champaigne's EX-VOTO *("Constipated")*. Delacroix does not seem to enchant him; at least, it is without warmth that he says of THE DEATH OF SARDANAPALUS: *"A real Western!"*

I try to find the line of taste which expresses itself through these preferences and aversions. But it is just like my companion: not easy to follow. He does not seem to look with his eyes, but with his whole body, so that one never knows whether he is seeing or dreaming. He is not dreaming. Before Linard's BASKET OF FLOWERS he says: *"There are some flowers, in there, that look as if they didn't want to get crushed."*

His gait is hardly less disconcerting. He does not walk, he drifts, headlong, head sunk into his shoulders, hands in his pockets. When he stops, one would swear he was rooted to the spot, but while one struggles to understand what made him immobilize himself, he silently goes and plants himself elsewhere. Half the time, it's not him but some German tourist I speak to. Every so often, I have the impression of grasping the thread. Before the sketch of THE SACRIFICE OF ABRAHAM by Rubens: *"Superb! I used to make sketches of those Rubenses, also of El Greco, Tintoretto. To get the freedom they had."*

Enchanted, I start to set up a genealogical tree of the emancipated touch, the free gesture: the Venetians, Rembrandt, Velásquez, Rubens, Hals. . . . Just then, we come to one of Hals' canvases: Scowl: *"He's a bore. Hals never holds up."*

There goes my tree, felled. I would suffer the same misadventure several more times. Looking at the Cézannes in the Jeu de Paume (that advanced wing of the Louvre where we now went, for the pleasure of crossing the Tuileries gardens) , I say to him: "These can't have mattered much to you."

"Because of his Cubism, you mean, and my rejection of geometrical construction? But that doesn't mean a thing. The essential quality is the same in all those who matter."

The essential quality? The present, or rather the presence of which it is the only threshold. Presence without identity. And I begin at last to understand that Riopelle's apparent illogic is the effect of his acute awareness of the opposition between that presence and that same logic. I was searching, without realizing it, for the well-made ear. I was forgetting its devilish adeptness at abandoning a form that can no longer deceive to reincarnate itself in the knife that cuts it off. What bothers Riopelle in Hals is that his touch acts like an end in itself. Systematic liberty is a systematic slavery that is not self-aware: one thinks of those serfs of insubmission, described by Alfred Jarry, who are punished if they do not disobey. Riopelle has a phobia of the systematic, as others suffer from claustrophobia.

"Norms are disastrous. They tried to justify the golden number and the rules by citing the beauty of ancient monuments. But if they reconstructed those monuments according to these rules, they would be pitiful, horrible!"

It is the spirit of system that repels him in Seurat, in Gauguin. His eye darts between the latter's HAY-MAKING IN BRITTANY and Van Gogh's GYPSY CAMP.

"That harmony in green," he says, designating the HAYMAKING, *"he wanted it, and he got it. In the* CAMP, *next to it, there is an exploding green, and it is the sky."*

A little farther on, before a landscape that actually is very washed-out, the BRETON VILLAGE IN THE SNOW, he says:

"If one didn't know that was a Gauguin, if it weren't signed, one would never guess it. He had to flaunt his style, his personality, in order to become known and recognized."

Then, as if the very flatness of his negation called for a corrective, he adds:

"There are very few Gauguin paintings that I like,

but those that I do like, I like as much as paintings by artists who are much closer to me in their attitude. One must judge a work by its intensity."

Nothing is acquired; or rather, that which is acquired is nothing. The success of one canvas is no guarantee for those which follow. Of Baugin's STILL-LIFE WITH CHESS-BOARD, he says:

"Very beautiful, but we see what he wanted to do and why he did it that way. On the other hand, DESSERT WITH GAUFRETTES defies understanding."

For him, there is no great body of work, there are only great works. One canvas, provided he recognizes the essential presence in it, is enough to make him like a painter; no matter how mediocre the rest of the work may be, his esteem will hardly vary. The present, the presence do not belong to the order of coherence, of continuity. He contemplates the great series of paintings dedicated by Rubens to Marie de Médicis. His gaze stops at THE LANDING:

"It is different from the others. The red draperies above the naiads are in the right place, are alive. In the others the red draperies are inert."

In fact, almost everywhere throughout the great room, made unnecessarily funereal by the pompous pseudo-Flemish frames, spots of the same garnet-red hand like the sails of becalmed ships. THE LANDING, stirred by an inexplicable wind, seems all the more unusual. The mastery, the assurance, which in the subjective realm are what rules and norms are in the objective, encumber more than aid:

"The real painting is the one which is a beginning. A guy who says, 'I do such and such well,' will begin to do it badly starting from that precise moment."

He uses expression "the real painting," and not "the beautiful painting," as if beauty implied a reference, however veiled, to some model, and therefore looked to the past:

"What matters is not to make a beautiful painting, but to make something progress."

"Just now, however, you were maintaining that there was no evolution in the realm of the essential."

"To progress is to destroy what you thought you had acquired."

Man is a clock that tends to run late and must constantly be set forward to the correct time. Occasionally we succeed in this, but by the time we have congratulated ourselves about it, we are already behind again. I am reminded of this passage from *Through the Looking-Glass:*

> "Well, in *our* country," said Alice, still panting a little, "you'd generally get to somewhere else— if you ran very fast for a long time, as we've been doing."
>
> "A slow sort of country!" said the Queen. "Now, *here,* you see, it takes all the running *you* can do, to keep in the same place. If you want to get somewhere else, you must run at least twice as fast as that!"

The Queen's country? The land of arts, of poetry. To progress, there, is to keep oneself in the present. (That is why all the works that succeed in this reveal the same time, the same essential place.)

"Art is not a revolt, and yet it is made up of revolts. Van Gogh is as classical as Vermeer."

Riopelle, a native of the Queen's country (well isn't he Canadian?), moves about it effortlessly; trying to keep up with him, I, who am from Alice's neighborhood, soon am panting a little, and rather disoriented. But I still was not prepared to have him declare, pointing to Baugin's DESSERT WITH GAUFRETTES:

"There's my man. That's what painting is. He takes the subject matter into account more than the others. The tablecloth is blue, so he paints it blue. He does not

eliminate things that bother him. He does not give the impression of composing. Not a shadow of prejudice. For me, this painting has the qualities of the VIEW OF DELFT: *it does not have the look of having been done, only of being there."*

Attraction of opposites? Spirit of contradiction or wish to disconcert? It is going to happen again.

"My heart goes out to Courbet's big canvases," he says. *"He looked at everything in detail. So much so that he drowned himself in them, and thereby found the essential."*

And we stop a long time before Degas' little dancer, the one with the real crumpled tutu and the faded ribbon in her waxy hair.

"How does it happen that you, who date your life as an artist from the day you renounced the image, have such an interest in those who lend it the most weight, the realists?"

He shrugs his shoulders, says nothing.

"All right, all right, a painter's heart has its reasons. . . . Anyhow, what astonishes me is not that you like Baugin, Potter, Courbet or Vermeer, but that you should say: *'How real that painting is, how alive that horse looks!'* And that THE CHATEAU OF ROSNY by Corot—undeniably marvelous—should wrest this comment from you: *'That's exactly how it is!'* I thought that you were interested in painting, not in well-made ears."

"An ear does exist, but not in itself, only in relation to the whole of the painting."

A painted face, or object, only lives through the life of the painting. If the painting lacks presence, the face or the object will seem inconsistent, unrealistic, however exact it may be. Riopelle laughs, looking at Berthe Morisot's THE HYDRANGEA, and points to the red spots in the lower right:

"What are they? Oranges, flowers? Luckily there is the title!"

Jean-Paul Riopelle: MAREMONT

Gustave Courbet: THE BURIAL AT ORNANS

In LOVE AND PSYCHE by Picot, he indicates the divine
seducer opening the alcove curtains to leave:

*"His hand, one can't quite believe it is holding the
curtain, it looks lighter than he is."*

It does not lack "correctness" but pictorial presence.
As proof, THE BATTLE by Uccello:

*"All those feet! He couldn't have known himself any
more whom they all belonged to. But what does it
matter? Everything functions: details, masses. It is
organic."*

Meaning: all is saturated with the life of the painting,
nothing is superimposed, nothing is far from this source.
We are before Manet's DÉJEUNER SUR L'HERBE:

"There is a lot of Courbet in it."

*"A lot of stopgap devices, too. The woman's foot in
the center seems to float because everything isn't
painted in that same style. On the other hand, there are
perfect parts: the still-life on the left, the blue coming
through the leaves, the little bird at the top. He was
also interested in the woman's blouse; but when he got
to her body, things weren't working any more. There
are too many intentions in this painting for the intensity to be sustained throughout."*

As a light goes on when the electric current reaches
a certain intensity, so the reality of things, on the canvas,
proclaims that of the painting. And yet this comparison
does not bring out enough the initial autonomy of the
two terms, and, once they are put into relation with
one another, the impulse which, in carrying them toward each other, causes each of them to go beyond itself
so that they merge, engendering a third term—*a
presence beyond the presence,* in Riopelle's words. The
passengers on a boat are irresistibly drawn to the bow
at the instant when an island, for a long time antici-
pated, suddenly appears: a moving synchrony, and so
perfect that one does not know if the island gives rise to
the looking or arises from it. Thus the vision joins and

overflows the thing seen and the person (painter or spectator) who sees it.

"*A Courbet trout is beautiful because one understands trout better after having seen it. And also because one understands painting better.*"

Riopelle, who, in renouncing representation, has reduced himself to the painting alone, nevertheless states:

"*For me, the only reference is nature. Freedom exists only there, and at the same time the strongest constraint. A tree can grow in only one way. There is no tragic, elegiac or joyous way to be a tree. There is only the right way.*"

Baugin's *gaufrettes,* just like the trees in the Tuileries, do not seem *made,* thought out, prepared, but *come about.* What Riopelle calls "nature," might it not be this emerging, this *élan,* which stirs the things of the world as well as the hand of the painter?

The birth of an island: few painters have offered us this experience as often as Manet. Riopelle lingers a long time before THE BALCONY:

"*This is one of the few things I really love.*"

He adds nothing, except to say, indicating the man dressed up in his false shirt front:

"*If you put a real necktie there, it wouldn't be more scandalous than that blue necktie in that green.*"

He judges ASPARAGUS to be "*superb*" but THE FIFE-PLAYER "*too well done.*" Of the WOMAN WITH FANS:

"*The movement from the arm to the fan, the dog— it's wild. . . . But the face is stiff, chalky. He doesn't want the painting to get away from him. He is afraid of himself.*"

About the portrait of Clemenceau:

"*This, yes! This was surely more within his scope than the* DÉJEUNER."

And there is Monet. We stop before THE REGATTAS AT

ARGENTEUIL, hanging between THE BASIN AT ARGENTEUIL and the GARE SAINT-LAZARE:

"Marvelous! This is the first modern painting I ever saw. The mast extending on into the water . . . He didn't stop to worry about the angle of refraction, the orientation of the sails or if the green of the boat reflected in the river was the right color. It came to him like that. He made time stand still to do his painting. The GARE SAINT-LAZARE, *on the contrary, is a problem painting—problem resolved, of course. The smoke in it is studied, not natural as is* THE BASIN AT ARGENTEUIL."

A number of paintings in the Jeu de Paume have been furnished with ridiculous frames. But the height of the grotesque has been achieved with the series of "Cathedrals" imbedded in the wall, which makes them look like color reproductions in a travel agency. And, supreme refinement, the granulation of the walls echoes that in the CATHEDRALS.

"It gives the impression that if you scraped the walls, you would find more Monets underneath."

"Yes, the supreme Cathedral where all the cathedrals would merge. After all, that's what he was looking for. In time, of course, not in space.

"What freedom from one to the other! And yet he neither varied his theme nor his style. Monet was the first to conceive a work in a series. I wonder if his cathedrals would hold up if one were to consider them separately."

One last look at Manet. The fascination he exercises over Riopelle is clarified. Where, in effect, does the inequality in this painter come from unless from the absence of a deliberately pursued system, from an affirmed confidence in the present? It does not follow that everything succeeds for him, but it does follow that the level of difference between failure and success is immediately apparent: noon is the most inexorable of reference points. Everything does not come to fruition, but what does is of an overwhelming freshness: at the end of experience, innocence recaptured. And one will note, without in the least diminishing Manet's genius, that historical coincidence made no small contribution to this good fortune. The image of the objective world and the imagizing, subjective world of the painter had been diverging for a long time. In Manet, they finally separated without, however, turning their backs on one another. The image is still necessary but no longer sufficient. A fault has opened between the deed and the doing, already deep enough for the painter to be unmistakably aware of it, not yet deep enough to prevent the establishment, from one bank to the other, of a unifying spark, a rapport.

But balance, in art, is the fruit of the unstable. Riopelle sighs:

"What would save us would be if there were a subject matter that didn't count too much, and a way of painting, of transposing, with no particular intrinsic value either. A system of symbols, what!"

In other words: that things—and their images—not be an end but the material manifestation of a transcendence which could also invest the painter, thus discharging him of the crushing obligation to confer a sense on these signs through his own powers alone. The place taken by a god in the world and in the painter creates in them a void which, unless man considers it an assurance, a given quantity rather than a quality to conquer, lessens and alleviates them, restricts but thus allows them to *overflow*.

If Riopelle has any regrets, they do not make him cling. One who is pledged to the present knows more than another that time is passing. The image, for his generation, had become nothing but a dead weight. He broke off because the break had become necessary.

Breaking was not, for all that, enough. And this is

what distinguishes Riopelle from most of the others who, during the same period, joined with him in their submission to an absolute present, without memory. Their *élan* derived from their desire to break with history—thus the obstacle speeds up the current—more than to abandon themselves to that part of the self which is our access to the now. For Riopelle, the break was the effect of his intransigeant aspiration toward the present; for them, it was the cause, the guarantee, the recipe. In attaching too much importance to the act of abolishing the image, they fell asleep in the conviction that everything had been done once that act had been accomplished. They painted spots as earlier they had painted ears. The present is unnamable; the names and forms the past assumes are numberless. Tomorrow new systems will solicit their unwitting servitors. They will abandon non-figuration all the more readily because it had exacted a cruelly radical attitude from them. With the image removed, they had only themselves to fall back on: it was too little, and history caught them up once more. There they are, those who were only in the present by coincidence, back in the imperfect again.

Riopelle, who had never granted that revolution an intrinsic virtue, remains faithful to it because no new lively rapport between the self and the world, the painter and the image, has yet presented itself to him. One who has painfully suffered the death of his ancient gods is not quick to kneel before new ones. The rejection of the past belongs to history, but sometimes it opens onto the experience of the present, which is intemporal, intimate. Noon, the present time, is the only time that strikes on two clocks. Those who know how to seize this fleeting chance often seem, from history's point of view, to immobilize themselves; from the other point of view, on the contrary, their creative impulse seems unflagging. It is not enough, in fact, not to be

late: one must also scale the dizzy hand of noon. The Fauves, the Nabis would turn to other modes of expression: Matisse and Bonnard would stand firm, without fear of getting out of style. In their fashion, Riopelle will have to resign himself to going ahead in solitude.

But even fidelity can become a betrayal. A change of theme or system allows one, if not to renew oneself, at least to stave off the moment when we must pay the bill. That is no longer possible for the painter whose work is not the product of a rapport with the representational world, but only with the forces of his own being. Then it is no longer the world that he is inventorizing; he is repeating himself. The fate of a painter pledged to the present is a difficult one, so exposed is he to seeing it elude him and so conscious of the slightest lapse back into the past!

Riopelle said to me one day:

"You never take more than one step in your life."

It is now more than fifteen years since he took that step and bound himself to it. The passage of time casts a pathetic light on his progress, as on a man who has based everything on youth. This is how it looks when I observe him from the point of view of history. But suffice it for the present to be caught up with one more time, and this tragic perspective fades at once. One thinks of a tree (*"nature, my only reference"*) that suddenly shakes off black and sterile winter to burst into a bloom so wild it seems totally unprecedented: such freshness could only be, at each return, for the first time. In the realms of history and science, the steps add up; in the land of art, the same step, provided it is a decisive one, can and must be taken over and over again.

"The thing that's sort of troublesome about paintings you've seen a lot and love," Riopelle tells me as we leave the museum, *"is that you want to see the same painting you saw again. But it is not there, it does not exist any more. Why try to make comparisons? What counts is to start."*

Zao Wou-ki

We bow and scrape to each other before the double doors, the heaviest and most unwieldy in Paris. Forcing me with a peremptory gesture to precede him, he says:

"Let's not behave like a couple of Chinamen."

I would soon perceive, to my great regret, that he was not joking at all. For I must admit it: just now, on my way to the Louvre, I had been nursing a dream. I thought that I had my Wild Indian, my Turk, the stranger whose reactions would throw some new light on the old, too-familiar domain. There at last was to take place the absolute confrontation, not glossed over, from which inevitably naked, simple truths would emerge. Of course, I was not unaware that the man I had arranged to meet had left his native China quite some time ago, but China is so far away! It seemed impossible to me that one could, in a few years, inwardly overcome the distance separating Peking from Paris. I counted on the isolating force of that distance and watched for the first expressions, the first words from Zao Wou-ki the way those theologians, to prove that the language of the Bible was the most ancient in the world, would keep a newborn baby away from all speech, convinced that the first words he would utter would be in Hebrew.

But my "newborn" knows the Bible by heart.

"Let's go and look at the Egyptian sculpture. On the way, we can see the Greek antiquities. Not the Roman sculpture: that is for people who like the Renaissance. Personally, it does not interest me."

And he adds, with a contrite smile, lowering his voice as if he were admitting a monstrous vice which nevertheless delighted him:

"I should not say it, but for me the Renaissance is the beginning of decadence."

Excusing himself for saying out loud what others have finally silenced by having proclaimed it too often —that is the very essense of exoticism. Excusing himself for speaking our language too well. Before Corot's THE STUDIO, with the girl in the red blouse:

"Degas learned a lot from that."

Before THE SUNKEN PATH by Ravier, a dark, tormented, heavily painted landscape: *"That is like the early Matisses, no?"* Or, about Chardin's still-lifes: *"I do not know why, in seeing them, I think of Cézanne."* And it is to punish me for my foolish hopes that he mockingly turns "yellow." Before the women bustling about at the feet of Tintoretto's SUSANNA AND THE ELDERS, he says very seriously: *"Is that a pedicure?"*

It is the breadth rather than the absence of his knowledge that betrays the stranger from a distant land. What Parisian has ever gone up the Eiffel Tower or been to the Folies-Bergère? What French painter would say to you today before a painting by Albert Besnard: *"He was my professors' professor"*? The foreignness is to be found at the heart of the familiarity itself—in an inflection, a misplaced accent. *"I like Cranach. It is the exact opposite of Oriental painting. Motionless, stiff."* Corot's GIRL READING brings a surprising exclamation from Zao Wou-ki: *"What bad taste!"* He finds THE WOMAN WITH THE PEARL and the portraits of children magnificent, *"but the landscapes do not touch me very much."* Before one of them, however, he indicates some branches with a delicate gesture and cries: *"Look at that! How did he do it? That is beautiful Chinese painting!"* And suddenly one understands: it is precisely the "Chinese" aspect of Corot that arouses his severe and at times rather cold reaction. One is always harder on the members of one's own family.

On the way to Egypt, this Kouros still all impregnated with its influence:

"In China, we knew nothing about the archaic Greeks. We only knew about the classic: the sixteenth and seventeenth centuries, and what they liked. Actually, we discovered the West through its most academic side. Careful workmanship. China today still likes finished things. Even a broken arm is offensive there."

The stele of Antoué:

"This mixture of image and writing pleases me. The details are mechanical, but the whole is pretty. The new parts are too beautiful. I like things better when they are a little damaged. The refinement is too studied, too

calculated. There are no surprises left. When you begin, you already know where you're going. In China, the Sung and Tang periods are full of surprises. Then, art became codified: the rising gesture . . ."

Stele of the Serpent-King:

"That is beautiful! Actually, the difference is an infinistesimal matter, but it is enough to distinguish the masterpiece from the mediocre."

"You seem to have a marked preference for geometrical works. A curious preference, at least if one thinks of your own painting."

"That is because I cannot be geometric myself. But I am less touched by the geometry of these simple tablets than by their extreme economy. The minimum of means for the maximum of ideas. A Sung painter said: 'I would like, when my brush touches the paper, my idea to have already gone beyond it.' A bad painter knows neither when to begin nor when to stop. Actually, the painting we like best today is the least overwrought, the least labored. The other kind is tiring."

He mentions his admiration for the Kanefer and Neferiret group, but makes a face before the CROUCHING SCRIBE:

"It is too . . ."

"Too what?"

"Too real."

On the other hand, the BEARER OF OFFERINGS enchants him:

"Delicate, but not complicated. Beautiful!"

And finally, before the SEATED OF THE ANCIENT EMPIRE:

"I love that marriage of painting and sculpture in Egyptian art. That perspective, that resonance."

One impression already prevails, which the rest of our tour will confirm. Zao Wou-ki's criterion is spontaneity. He is drawn toward what erupts and pours forth

with the unexpectedness and rightness of a spring. The rest is "tiring" despite the talent: Ingres, David. THE RAPE OF THE SABINES: *"Too equal everywhere. It is like the class photo. One can sense the teacher thinking: no favorites!"* Just think what it is like when the teacher is not a genius! Before Millet's THE ANGELUS: *"That is one of the first Western paintings that I saw in reproduction. The earth, the people, the sky, everything is painted the same. Are they the same, then—the ground, a leg, air? Funny!"*

Rigidity of viewpoint or stupidity, eloquence that forces the issue, imperviousness of genius: all infidelities to the wellspring that explains Zao Wou-ki's tastes and distastes. He prefers Fra Lippo Lippi to Botticelli, and Paolo Veneziano to Fra Angelico: *"Those marbles, that gold—in impeccable bad taste! It is a fussy, overworked painting. Of course, one can make a polished painting, but if we can see that the artist is getting tired, we get tired too. I would rather he had lifted a lighter weight than give me the feeling he was working himself to death."* Carracci bores, but not Caravaggio, La Tour or Vermeer. He says, further: *"I prefer Titian to Veronese. Veronese shows off too much. He is theatrical. His figures are posed. One might say the opera. Titian is more sincere."* He marvels at Courbet's great works (with a preference for THE STUDIO—*"One can breathe more freely, it is more intimate"*), but admits: *"Géricault does not touch me very much. It is a little like the movies"* (we are looking at THE PLASTER KILN). *"Ac-*

tually, all the Romantics are a little like the movies. With the exception of certain Delacroixs." On the contrary, it is the simplicity that seduces him in Giorgione's THE COUNTRY CONCERT, LA MARQUESA DE LA SOLANA by Goya, Watteau's THE INDIFFERENT, Rembrandt's BATHSHEBA: *"He only paints one color—golden brown—but he is never tiring."* As for THE DISCIPLES AT EMMAÜS: *"Light itself! Incredible that a man could do that. When one enters, one is drawn to that painting like a moth to a candle."* And, about Tintoretto's self-portrait, he says: *"It is done with nothing. The richest thing is the frame."* Transparency, light: the noncaptive quality, effusive, trembling like a shrimp that has just shed its shell. The light of a Monet landscape (hanging in the Salle des Réserves), the virginal light of Vermeer: *"The touch, the transparency are a little reminiscent of Poussin."* We are standing before Poussin's canvases, which bad luck has relegated to the darkest part of the Grande Gallerie:

"He is a poet. What enchantment! There is the joy of painting. One has the impression that he is so happy to be painting that he trembles before the canvas."

Effusion does not mean vagueness, and the unexpected is not gratuitous at all. Before Mantegna's CAL-VARY:

"Marvelous! The way of treating the mountains: it is as though they were engraved, sliced by a sharp ax. Every detail stands out, but there is a unity to it, and it is not tiring. One has the impression that it was all done in one breath."

Goliath can bring his crushing weight to bear anywhere; David, however, must strike accurately: precision is the salvation of sensibility. Titian's WOMAN AT HER TOILET: *"Have you noticed the white spot in the black mirror?"* Uccello's BATTLE: *"The horses are modeled like jointed manikins. The figures are like engraved steel. And all those lances! They are the most beautiful thing. In the painting in Florence, there are rosebushes on the battlefield."*

The rose and the lance: certainty of the present and assurance of the future.

The preoccupation with the future is the origin of another series of remarks. Zao Wou-ki looks closely at the PORTRAIT OF AN ARTIST by Géricault:

"The black always crackles a little. The blues do not change at all. Ivory black is a troublesome color, as I found out at my own expense."

"Then why do you use it?"

"Because no color has such intensity."

At first glance, the preoccupation with technique (which makes a work endure) seems incompatible with the preoccupation with spontaneity (which makes it live). Zao Wou-ki seems to recognize this when he says,

Zao Wou-ki: UNTITLED PAINTING

Giovanni Cimabue: VIRGIN WITH ANGELS

about a very heavily painted landscape by Huet: *"That is a little too much like a ceramic."* In reality, it is spontaneity that leads to the most effective technical treatments. Zao Wou-ki points to Prud'hon's JUSTICE AND DIVINE VENGEANCE PURSUING CRIME: *"The faces are crackled, but not the sky. Why? Because he worked on the sky less."*

Thus, the immediate and the permanent are deeply allied. In one breath, before Corot's WOMAN WITH THE PEARL:

"What freshness, what strength! One has the impression that this work has been cooking for millions of years. In China, they boil herbs over a very low flame for years to make them better."

And in Courbet, too, it is the alliance of the rose with steel that he calls attention to. The little REMISE (ROES' HIDEOUT) hung in the Salle des "Réserves."

"What nerve!" [A pause.] *"It is like the ancient bronzes. Solid, not thick. It has the feeling of a painting that has just been born and yet has endured for centuries."*

Effusion, precision, lightness, strength all call and answer one another. How define the role of one or the other in Cimabue's VIRGIN WITH ANGELS?

"This is the most beautiful thing in the Louvre. That serenity: everything is almost on the same level, but the gold halos create a strange perspective, planes. It makes me think of ancient Chinese landscapes, where the banks of fog separate the planes. The outline of the wings and the throne, the frame: what prodigious composition! Generally, they blocked off things in the early paintings: here one would say that it opens up. The Renaissance made the subject matter stand out against the background—in Western painting the subject matter has killed many things; here, one cannot detach the subject matter from the background. All the things, on the bottom—the feet of the throne, the angel's foot—

*make the painting live: one does not think about feet.
The gold makes holes in the painting, and these holes
allow the painting to breathe. They are like springs."*

Like springs at the bottom of a lake whose clarity
they constantly renew and level they maintain at full-
ness.

One of the surest signs of spontaneity is that it
eludes influences. Now, Zao Wou-ki has been subjected
to twice as many influences as most artists.

*"In the seventeenth century, an Italian became the
Emperor's official painter. He introduced chiaroscuro,
volume, Western perspective: only the composition remained Chinese. The Chinese were enraptured: 'Ah,
how alive it is! How real!' Today, there are even some
imbeciles who say that Chinese painting is not scientific. Chinese painters came to study official art in Paris.
That led to something like Russian painting: Meissonier, Luc Simon and the like. My uncle, who studied at
the Sorbonne, brought me back postcards showing the
works of Prud'hon, Picot, etc. They were the first that
I had seen. At the National Beaux-Arts School in Han
Tcheou, they taught us all the worst things the West
had to offer. They made us draw Greek plaster casts."*

"You make me think of the little Congolese children
who knew the names of French rivers better than the
ones in their own country."

*"Oh! They also taught us our own rivers! For along
with the Western system, they taught us Chinese-style
perspective. They showed us Sung landscapes. But the
play of ink and water is not enough. We did not know
where we were any more. Some of us leaned in one
direction, some in the other. Oil, water: we were doubly
academic. In truth, painters trained like this are only
fit for painting propaganda."*

"Didn't you try to liberate yourselves?"

*"Of course. We engaged in a little Fauvism. Think
about it: ever since the fifteenth century, we had lost*

color. All we had left was atmosphere. Fauvism seemed acceptable to us because of the role the line plays in it. On the other hand, Cubism just would not do. It was a deciphering, a code art, while we were involved in feeling and projecting.

"*So I made a sort of Fauvism based on reproductions I had found in* Life, Vogue, *and also in Japanese magazines. I cut out all these pictures and glued them into a big bound scrapbook. I spent my Sundays doing that. I liked Cézanne, Renoir, Modigliani. Modigliani, with his elongated line, is very easy for a beginner. I also liked Picasso. None of this was very serious. There were no professors to help us, no ambiance. In 1936, the war broke out. The school kept moving all the time, with the Japanese in pursuit. This artistic stagnation lasted for six years.*"

After the war, the call of the West became irresistible. "*I had learned the Western style: it was normal to go there.*" That may be. But was there not also a need to get closer to that flame which is always changing place and school—as if to force us to understand that no place, no school possesses it—that flame which then seemed to be centered in Paris?

"*I came directly to Paris, arriving April 1, 1948, at eight o'clock in the morning. That same afternoon, I was at the Louvre. I can still remember that visit. Too many things to see! I was lost. Like everyone else, I latched on to the* MONA LISA. *Certain painters—Botticelli, Fra Angelico—disappointed me: I liked them better in reproduction. All those constipated Madonnas!*

"*I went to the Louvre all the time. A half day of French lessons, a half day of museum and exhibitions. At night, I would draw (I was not painting any more). I did this for a year and a half. I traveled a lot. From morning to night, I visited museums. Madness! Even the most insignificant little Gothic churches, in Italy . . .*"

Strange way of liberating oneself!

"It's that it is not easy to break free. Everybody is bound by a tradition—I, by two. To make a good painting, you have to understand. The young Van Gogh liked some very, very bad painters."

But how to understand what does not belong inside the horizons of one's own culture? When the knowledge of a language is lost, we can only admire the strength or grace of the signs it has left on a stele, or on a manuscript. This superficial experience was a betrayal at the time when the signs had roots in the intellectual, social and religious fabric of those who drew them, but is not one today, when the fate of the painting is played out on the surface. Aesthetics, because it detaches the work from its roots, is a universal language: postcards go everywhere, and quickly. Abstraction, which we know is the ultimate consequence of that long climb which, since the Venetians, has progressively brought painting to coincide with its surface, abolishes the secret layers through which paintings used to differentiate themselves.

"I see the paintings in the Louvre much more clearly now that I am abstract. I can discern the painter's real intentions better. The good sides of Corot and Courbet stand out more clearly. One sees the essential. I think that Corot wanted to make a beautiful painting, not a beautiful tree."

The accelerated apprenticeship to the West lasted a year and a half.

"Then, I felt like painting. I had wanted to be wised up, and I was. I said to myself: to work! I came back to the Louvre from time to time. Less and less frequently. I was painting. In China, I had already tried to make 'modern' paintings without understanding. I kept the drawings of my little sister, who was about seven or eight. I copied her, I thought that she was freer than I was. I came across Klee by chance, around 1945, and found that his work had a certain rapport with what my sister's drawings had made me feel. That drew me toward him. Klee was a means of knowing nature other than the academic way. It is not so much his way of painting that is modern, as his way of seeing."

Zao Wou-ki's painting, today, seems to be born of itself. Emotion is its source; the end of emotion its form. Elsewhere he says: *"Everyone is bound by a tradition—I, by two."* Impossible? But the work exists, and Zao Wou-ki has just given many proofs of his double culture.

So we are obliged to remind ourselves of a simple truth: that there are two innocences. The first, the more generally accepted, is before knowledge. It is also the more fragile. Those who deny or ignore history are its first victims. Naïve painters are incapable of resisting the intentions or qualities we attribute to them. A period revolted by its own culture "invents" its naïve artists. They are placed in the margin, which is determined by the text. The second innocence arises, sometimes, beyond knowledge. Hence it is no longer at its mercy. This is the nature of a Zao Wou-ki's spontaneity.

But how can such an impressionable man have escaped his influences? Not by refusing them but by accepting them all. The West liberates him from the East, the East saves him from the West. Between the

two, he builds his empire of the middle. Zao Wou-ki's place is the zone—hardly more than a pinpoint—that one has never reached, that one has never left: the place one passes through. Everything is in suspension, light, delicate, precise and precarious, like the rip, the unique fringe that forms when the waters of a river meet those of the ocean. Zao Wou-ki rides this unstable crest with virtuosity. The wave can break, tumbling those it carries: thus the Flemish Mannerists of the sixteenth century, at the limits of the spheres of influence of the Flemish Primitives and the Italian Renaissance. Not so long ago, a traveler whose papers were not in order found that all the countries where his boat landed refused him the right to come ashore; he was forced to spend several years at sea. Zao Wou-ki, for his part, has chosen not to disembark any more. And in the same way that white is the result of all colors, Zao Wou-ki's abstraction flows from the complete acceptance of representations that counteract each other.

An instinctive or deliberate need to contradict one's natural bent, because the essential is not that bent, but what arises from the tension:

"I tell myself that I am not a landscapist. I refuse to let the landscape into my studio. But truthfully, perhaps that is because it enters more easily than anything else."

The privileged state is that of passage, of suspension,

where the work is no longer an emanation of subjectivity and is not yet an object:

"A canvas for me is good when I can make another one right afterward. A bad painting is when you are blocked."

Excess is an end, but the middle ground is only alive on the condition that it is not a consequence of moderation: it must be born of the confrontation of extremes.

And I think of Zao Wou-ki's recent canvases, of his faculty for changing—in the wink of an eye: the wink needed to grasp the possibility of a passage—changing the silent patience into prompt and infallible action. Broader, more tumultuous than before, they make the singular nature of his temperament stand out all the more clearly. For a closely woven texture of values leaves the painter a certain room for maneuver; marked contrasts, on the contrary, only allow for shrill, lightning passages. Dramatic life is born of these neuralgic points, where the contradictory elements reverse themselves, convert themselves into each other. Sometimes, the drama is concentrated in more than a few points: each zone, one by one, is the hinge around which the others pivot and emerge again. It is the painting as a whole that becomes the passage.

It evokes a heavy sky and a leaden sea, so dissimilar that the horizon line seems to confirm an irremediable rupture. But a sudden, impalpable condensation makes them communicate, and the movement begins again, the cycle of life is saved. Zao Wou-ki knows how to capture the moments, delicate and exact as a precision scale, of concentration and deconcentration, without which all would be but duality, rupture, inertia. The airy landscape condenses into a rain of signs. Shall we be able to read them? No, already they are only ripples in a liquid universe. Along the way, color becomes less and less ponderous, until it is nothing but light, gesture grows heavier, until it is nothing but form. The touch is now long, diluted, serene; now short, exacerbated, loaded. Here the paintbrush seems to be manipulated from the wrist, there at arm's length. The heavy wave throws foam toward the sky where it catches the sun, turns into pearls, falls back again and melts into the water once more. And the essential is not the sum of these states, or one among them, but their aptitude for perpetual metamorphosis.

Neither painting-project nor painting-object. Neither beginning nor end. The work is situated where things are alive, which is to say, where they pass. Freedom, but freedom made of minutely measured servitudes. If Zao Wou-ki has a gift for making antagonistic worlds coexist, it is because he knows the art of keeping his balance at the heart of disequilibrium itself, on the beam of the scale. Neither the West nor the East has taught him this sharpness. He had it in him, but thanks to them, he was able to recognize it. And so now their role seems, at least in so far as he is concerned, to have been fulfilled. As we leave the Louvre, Zao Wou-ki says to me:

"I am no longer curious at all."

Marc Chagall

Marc Chagall took the walk we are about to begin fifty-seven years ago for the first time. It was the day after he arrived in Paris in 1910.

"I hurried at once to the Salon des Indépendants (the Salon d'Automne was for successful artists) . I went quickly to the moderns, at the far end. There were the Cubists: Delaunay, Gleizes, Léger. . . . And then, I raced to the Louvre. A magic name . . ."

"Why to the Louvre?"

"I felt that the truth was there. The moderns hadn't passed the test yet. There, it was serious."

"The test of time?"

"No, not time. Something else . . ."

Fifty-seven years ago, but the memory is still clear:

"Way up, in the Grande Galerie, I discovered Bassano's big painting. A mixture of people and animals. I sensed that it was very important."

Beyond a doubt, the Louvre had shown him, as a welcome, a kind of Chagall. The dream of the self-educated adolescent from Vitebsk, then, did have an equivalent in the pictorial tradition of the Latin West. The undertaking became possible. The museum as a school? It does not seem so:

*"I go to the Louvre to fortify myself, control myself.
One hopes to learn something, but it is no use. Nothing
helps us. There are no assurances, no certitudes. Learn?"*
He laughs. *"Nothing! One does not learn how to paint.
I am against the well-drawn, the well-painted. Cézanne
had no draftsmanship, nothing."*

Is not that precisely what the Louvre is? Here, time
and place no longer exist; there are no more fathers,
sons, or brothers; no more causes, or effects. He says:

"It is the cemetery for genius."

But what he means by that is that the work, behind
the frontier marked by the museum, is snatched from
history, released.

"Death helps one to see a great deal."

Thus the adventure would be very simple. A dream,
so intimate that it occurs in the margin of history, encouraged by the encounter with a work that owes nothing more to time, materializes. A symbol of such a conjuncture: at this very moment, Chagall is being
exhibited at the Louvre.

In fact, he seems to have foiled the ravages of time,
like a refugee who has eluded a hundred police round-
ups. This man of eighty years and more is possessed of a
stupefying physical vigor and mental vivacity. His eyes
are now mocking, now tender, his smile ready, his step
and speech rapid. There are people who polish themselves little by little until they become their own myth.

What makes of Chagall a legendary being—passers-by recognize him and ask for his autograph—on the contrary, is that he simply has not changed. An uninterrupted childhood, because nourished exclusively by his dreams. All attention to his interior monologue, as Harpo Marx, whom Chagall resembles a little, is silent in his films. Angels do not age.

Simple, too simple. Chagall's eyes are wide open.

"I see things. I am a terrible, a formidable critic. Ever since 1910, I have rarely been wrong. Except about Rouault: he bored me."

I admit that I was skeptical, at first: criticism must be able to bite. But as we wended our way along the quays, our conversation convinced me: the angel has teeth.

"Bonnard? A beefsteak that has been handled too much. 'Finger painting.' A little bourgeois. A man who does not look you straight in the eye. Matisse, yes! That rousing anarchy, that dash!"

"You have never been wrong, you say?"

"Yes, of course. I believed in Gleizes too much. I saw in him a sort of Courbet of Cubism. Today, I have a higher opinion of Delaunay at the time when he was modest than later, when he was pushing himself. He used to reproach me: 'Chagall, you don't know the tricks of the trade.' But he knew them. And yet, today, I notice, his work is falling apart. On the other hand, I used to think: La Fresnaye, he is a nice artist; now, he has gained scope."

This is because then Chagall was immersed in history, which is always unjust:

"I saw the chemical difference between Picabia and Léger very clearly, but it didn't matter much. The closer you get to your times, the less close you feel. Even Corot seemed too realistic to me during that period. Monet, I did not want to look at him. I discovered him after the war, on the boat that brought me back from

America. There, on the ocean, I asked myself the question: whose color really pours forth naturally? And I answered: Monet. Today, for me, Monet is the Michelangelo of our times, from the chemical point of view."

History's attenuation liberates clearsightedness, as one can only see that a lamp is lighted after sundown. On the condition, naturally, that it is burning.

"I can tell if you were born with a voice or not. There is no professionalism. The technique employed means nothing. Dadaism is not so great, but Schwitters made some marvelous works."

Chagall has a name for that lighted lamp, that critical mind:

"In our own times, the eye does not work very well. We do not see the differences. We do not see the chemistry. But later, we see it automatically. Because it alone exists. Watteau endured for us not because of his figures, but because of chemistry. Pater has the same figures, but he has not endured. Today, for me, there is chemistry. All the rest—realism or anti-realism, figuration or non-figuration—no longer matters."

Well, then, why can we not see clearly right off, why not turn on in art that second lighting which extinguishes everything that is not what Chagall calls "chemistry"? Because it is not possible.

"To arrive at that, at the Louvre, I told myself that we had to overthrow what was before us, which was the realisms."

The road to lucidity necessarily passes through its opposite. A god is only omnipotent in relation to man, and the untemporal is born of time. The lamp of second sight can only light itself at the blinding fire of history. Despite his personal, historical, geographical and cultural distance from the Parisian milieu which greeted him in 1910, Chagall at once and instinctively understood this: before going to the Louvre, he ran to the Salon des Indépendants. A simple phrase, spoken in passing, says more on this subject than lengthy explanations:

"I am the same age as Juan Gris."

At five minutes to ten, outside the great Denon Door, which is the main entrance, the crowd is already forming.

"The Louvre, what a magic word! Going to the Louvre is like opening the Bible or Shakespeare. Of course, there are some boring things. Guido Reni is a pompier *but a* pompier *of great class."*

"Is there a spirit of the place?"

"Without any doubt. Transport the Louvre to the Trocadéro and it would lose everything. The Louvre is a magical thing. It has to do with the proportions, the architecture of the galleries. Even its shadows are propitious. The walls are extraordinary. At the Metropolitan Museum, at the National Gallery in Washington, you won't find this magic. At the Hermitage, yes. A large part of the fascination that the Louvre has for artists comes from this."

"There are those, however, who dream of burning it down."

"What for? Those who are inside it are just people like us. They had the good luck, or the bad luck, to get into the Louvre; that's all. Anyhow, half of them might have to get out again. The risk of destruction is not there."

"Where, then?"

"In the 'museographic' hanging, which smacks of vandalism. I don't like the way the Louvre has been reorganized very much. It is no longer recognizable. I loved those paintings that used to climb in serried ranks up to the moldings. Everything was on a par. It was intimate. Now the tendency is to put a single painting on one wall. They impose what should be seen, they emphasize. The isolated painting, set apart, says: respect me. I like to look, to find."

And Chagall informs me that while he has never stopped going to the Louvre, ever since 1910, it has always been by chance—or at least seemingly so. The other day, when I suggested that the two of us make this visit, he answered:

"Yes, but I don't want to go on purpose."

I was a little annoyed, I admit: the demand seemed to me not only impossible to satisfy but also gratuitous. But was it? In the form of a game, Chagall was presenting me with the problem that had been his own: how does one cultivate ingenuousness? The paradox was a parabole. And indeed the solution did exist since, at that very moment, we were entering the doors of the Louvre.

Chagall pulls me up the staircase opposite the one dominated by the WINGED VICTORY and along toward the enormous suite of rooms on the second floor that harbors the juggernauts of French painting. Surprise: without the slightest hesitation his gaze travels to the

canvases of a painter I imagined would be at opposite
poles from his own nature, Courbet:

*"He is an artist I am passionate about. Of the same
breed as Masaccio, as Titian."*

His eye wanders around the immense hall, stopping
for an instant on THE RAFT OF THE MEDUSA:

"Yes, even STAGS FIGHTING, *which is a little academic,
touches me more than Géricault and his technique. Of
course, it is eloquent; and Gros, too, with his* BATTLE OF
EYLAU, *is quite something. But I don't feel like endors-
ing him, all the same. In the whole room, Courbet is
the one who stands up."*

"Why?"

*"I don't know. He moves me. To tears, almost. He is
the artist of life."*

He is standing before THE STUDIO:

"Somewhere, there, is the tragedy of death."

Against their background, a fog of variable density,
are light or dark groups, like pulsations:

*"Time, which comes, which goes, like a wave. We are
shadowy. That is our sickness."*

Now Chagall is before THE BURIAL AT ORNANS.
Chagall? I have trouble recognizing him. The voice is
neutral, the speech precise, the eye active. He speaks,
falls silent, steps back, moves closer, says something
more, as an artist returns to his easel to place another
brushstroke on his canvas:

*"That sickliness, that execution, those faltering yet
solid forms . . . I think of Braque: he could not do a*

bird properly, he would add some white, but that white!
. . . Courbet's whites; the dog, the hats are vivid spots.
And the blue of the man's stockings in the foreground:
it is apart, not linked to the rest. It is very modern. . . .
The enormous poetry of our times . . . Courbet is a
naturalist, and yet he is a great poet. . . . The idea of
death is everywhere in Courbet: it is not in Delacroix
and Géricault, although they treated the theme of
death."

After a fairly long silence, during which, at Chagall's
suggestion, I think about the strange marriage of energy
and decay in Courbet, he says:

"Perfection is close to death. Watteau, Mozart . . ."

And then, as we are heading for the transitional
rooms where the paintings from the Beistegui Collection are hung, Chagall adds:

"Courbet was right when he turned toward reality.
As for myself, I do not understand myself. I only know
one thing: my paintbrush is guided from my belly. It is
the guiding of the paintbrush that counts."

Now we are before LUCRETIA by Rubens, another in
the family of vigorous, exuberant artists:

"He is a pig, but he is a great artist."

He does not linger at all. David, on the other hand,
attracts him. Here is the unfinished NAPOLEON:

"I like it when paintings are left empty. . . . David
has a delightful touch." His gaze shifts to the Ingres
portraits, very close by. *"It is better than Ingres. A*
nobility. It is not dry, like Ingres." He indicates the

PORTRAIT OF MADAME DE VERNINAC: *"A delightful gray. What softness in the background!"*

We come to the thick-set MADAME PANCKOUKE by Ingres:

"He is more secretive, antinatural, abnormal. David is normal. Ingres disturbs me. There is something over-stuffed about him. There is a sort of impotence in his portraits. They seem overworked, chiaroscuro. One thinks of Magritte." A pause. *"If one has an academic soul, one has had it since birth."*

In front of Delacroix's PORTRAIT OF CHOPIN:

"A great work. The great Delacroix is there. It is almost a Soutine."

And at Delacroix's SELF-PORTRAIT:

"One really senses that Manet will come. What intelligence!"

A glance at the Chassériau that happens to be there on a temporary basis (they have removed several paintings by Ingres to send them to the Centennial Exhibition):

"A sort of La Fresnaye. He began with tricks."

He hastens over to Géricault's MAD WOMAN, which also replaces an Ingres portrait:

"There, this is the great Géricault. When Géricault painted reality, he was a great madman. When he made THE RAFT OF THE MEDUSA, *he was carrying out a plan. . . . One has to have a great deal of strength to sit down before a head and make a study of it."*

Farther on, the halls leading to the Grande Galerie occupied by the foreign collections. Chagall does not want to go there. He seems to prefer the French school today. I lead him, almost by force, to Goya's LA MAR-QUESA DE LA SOLANA, framed by the Davids and Ingres:

"It is like a Watteau—but no: it is not from our country. Like Velásquez. One can weep before Courbet and Watteau, but not before Velásquez or Goya. They are gods, but foreign gods. Zurbarán perhaps—such freshness! And Greco—but he was Greek. There is always that bullfight quality: this Goya succeeds like a moment of truth."

He turns away immediately to look at MADAME DE VERNINAC again:

"That yellowish liquid, what nobility! It is the café crème *one dreams about in foreign countries. I like that gray better than Goya's superb gray. That is what I left Russia for."*

This preference for French painting, since the beginning of our tour, is full of significance. Transposed in time and space, it re-enacts the young twenty-year-old's choice in leaving Vitebsk for Paris.

"My training has been French. I detest the Russian or Central European color. Their color is like their shoes. Soutine, myself—we all left because of the color. I was very dark when I arrived in Paris. I was the color of a potato, like Van Gogh. Paris is light."

Chagall's attraction to French painting, so steady, so positive, may seem strange. His temperament should have carried him to Vienna, Munich, or some Tahiti closer to the Dnieper than to the Seine. In fact, his first canvases, painted under the influence of Western works known to him only through reproductions in magazines, illustrate his affinities for a subjective art. Yet, instinctively, Chagall chose the opposite, because it was the opposite. When, thanks to a scholarship procured for him by a deputy to the Douma, Vinaver, he arrived

in Paris in 1910, those who attracted him and soon surrounded him were Cendrars, Apollinaire, Léger, La
Fresnaye, Delaunay, Lhote, Gleizes—in other words,
the defenders of an objective, formalistic art. *"The
painters of thirty years ago were absorbed in purely
technical pursuits,"* he said about them. *"One did not
talk out loud about one's dreams."*

Why seek out that which goes against you? Why,
when you are in love with Bassano, run all the way to
the farthest room at the Indépendants? Necessity. *"So I
arrived in Paris as though driven by destiny,"* Chagall
wrote further. *"From my mouth flowed words straight
from my heart. They almost suffocated me. I stuttered.
The words came hurrying out, anxious to be illuminated by that Paris light, to be bathed in it."*

Elsewhere, Chagall called that light "freedom light."
Something very precise lies hidden beneath the happy
imprecision of the formula: the bringing to light, the
liberation of the interiority captive in the darkest
depths of the self. Paris offered Chagall what his stut-
tering dream needed to take shape: a pictorial language,
a syntax of the visible. Thanks to this encounter, Chagall escaped—as did Soutine—from what is the hell of
art in Central Europe and Russia, the hell of the voice
deprived of speech, described by Aeschylus in *Agamem-
non:* "In shadow, he groans in pain, without hope of
ever drawing anything from an interior on fire. . . ."

To take shape is to take root in history. The Indépendants and the Louvre: the path of every artist, even
the most secretive, passes through the art of his times.
The times, for the young Chagall, were the second
generation of Cubists. The essential fact is that he had

the wisdom to accept being the same age, in painting, as Juan Gris.

He needed courage for that. The Cubist language is materialistic, optical, general: Chagall's world is visionary, particular, local. The opposition seems, in this case, to border on incompatibility; expression and communication seem separated by all the distance there is between Vitebsk and Paris. No matter: as antagonistic as they were, only Paris could bring Vitebsk to light. Chagall did not like Cubism: he needed it.

"I detested realism and naturalism, even in the Cubists. I wanted to introduce a psychic formalism."

Meaning: the psychic could only become perceptible through a formalism. "I admit that two and two make four is an excellent thing," wrote Dostoevsky, "but if one must praise everything, I will tell you that two and two make five is also a charming thing." $2 + 2 = 4$ is Cubism's formula; $2 + 2 = 5$ is Chagall's. But that supernumerary 1, which is the sign of the fantastic, only emerges against a background of order, as a derogation to the logical permanence incarnated by the equation and its functioning. "Your monsters are viable," Louis Pasteur said to Odilon Redon. French painting offers visual viability to extrapictorial dreams.

"The Cubist bottles were straight: I leaned them over. I cut off heads. . . ."

The unreal manifests itself through a warping of the real, of that moment of realism that was Cubism. It was the defender of Cubism, Apollinaire, who first recognized the "surreal" in Chagall's Cubist-oriented work. But naturally, Chagall would take exception to the Surrealism developing when he returned to Paris after the war, in 1923.

"Surrealism is automatism. Art requires control, but by the artist's gift."

Obviously, Chagall illustrates in a fairly radical fashion the conflict between the self and society, between the personal voice and the common speech, which every

artist must resolve. On the one hand, the Russian cli-
mate, the Jewish milieu, the influence of Hasidism
(that sort of Hebrew Franciscanism), the dreamer's
temperament; on the other, the technicality of Cubism.
And thanks to Cubism, Chagall's work did not stay lost
in the limbo of formless reverie or the natural reserve
of folklore.

But he had yet to precipitate things: that was the
role of "chemistry." This is not the place to tell how
Chagall reinterpreted Cubism, making use of the right
it had won to dislocate and recompose forms in order
to topple heads and hoist the ox up onto the roof,
making Delaunay's orphic circle spin like the wheel of
chance at a street fair. Let us simply note that, for a
painter, to understand clearly is to misunderstand. His
false interpretation is in itself creative. Only the historian or the scholar can allow himself to be right.
Chagall's interpretation of Cubism reminds one of
what happened to the names of the Greek gods when
they passed from the universe of the archaic theogonies
into that of the pre-Socratic philosophies. At first
symbols of manifestations of the sacred, these names
lost their meanings as the gods died or were forgotten.
They became mysterious instead of clear, in such a way
that they were finally used as symbols of mystery, or
were attributed to powers still unnamed and as essential
as the gods whom they succeded.

The inventive artist is a wolf who presents himself to
us hidden, sometimes rather badly, in sheep's clothing.
When we see through the ruse, it is too late. Creation
is a-historic, but it must manifest itself in the bosom of
history. And one thinks of the fate of the Jew: escap-
ing from time but only discovering his exceptional
status by submitting to the rules of time, affirming his
difference by the very degree to which he assimilates
himself into his milieu—as French painting, in mask-
ing Chagall's universe, reveals it. To show oneself to
be different through the common language, to resolve

the paradox of the double belonging—the solution being precisely his work—is the artist's lot. Every creator is a Jew within his culture.

We retrace our steps through the French galleries, this time all the way to the Staircase of Honor. David's self-portrait:

"It is beautiful like Cézanne. It kills all of Ingres."

Delacroix, THE WOMEN OF ALGIERS IN THEIR APART-MENT:

"Magnificent, like his self-portrait. It moves me. His Raphaelesque folds are better than Courbet's. Courbet thought about death too much; he was an invalid."

Now we have come to the great neoclassical hall.

"Aie! Aie! Aie!" But he breathes freely again look-ing at THE RAPE OF THE SABINES and THE CORONATION OF NAPOLEON:

"No matter what he does, David is never academic. One is born academic. Neither Delacroix, nor Courbet, nor Géricault is—but Ingres."

Chagall's gaze wanders among the David canvases.

*"*MADAME RÉCAMIER, *marvelous. There is some Manet in it. But in* LEONIDAS, *there is Poussin. What softness, wrapped over everything! Never any dryness."* He points toward THE OATH OF THE HORACES.

No chemistry without acid:

"Perhaps I might not feel so tenderly toward David if people weren't talking about Ingres so much these days."

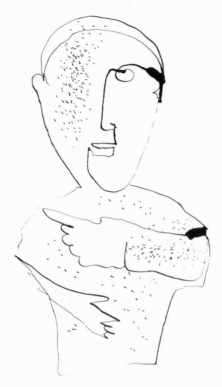

The Cimabue in the staircase. The tone changes, as
if we were passing from history to truth:

*"Cimabue! My love, my god! When I arrived in
Paris, it was a great shock."* Silence. *"It transcends everything. That devoutness . . . No, I am not talking
about the subject matter, but about the touch. Cimabue
is more penetrating than Giotto. . . . You have to go
to Watteau to find the equivalent. Rembrandt, Monet,
Caravaggio, Masaccio, Cimabue, Watteau, these are my
gods!"*

We descend the staircase. Passing before WINGED
VICTORY, Chagall whispers to me:

"It moves me more than Brancusi."

We pass a fresco, brought back from Ostia, HERO
ARMED WITH A SWORD:

*"This was done by a simple artisan. Art is like a good
child: it should not go to school. One must not try to*

draw well, *paint* well. *School is harmful. When I came to France, there was no professionalism in me. I had no mission. For me, that has not changed."*

A window, through which we glimpse the delicate gray of Paris. Chagall goes over to it:

"There is why we left Vitebsk. It is all of Le Nain, it is Watteau. The French are not always great, far from it, but there is this gray, this landscape in them. Fauvism can be as violent as it likes, it remains—in a Dufy, for example—French. Van Dongen has much more talent, but he vomits it."

Chagall is determined not to leave the French domain. Despite his age, despite the kilometers we have already covered, he drags me to the other end of the Louvre, way up high, where the new rooms for the eighteenth and nineteenth centuries are located, and again it is a David, MADAME TRUDAINE, that greets us:

"The touch, marvelous! He is perhaps the first to have used such a light touch. The execution, it's everything; it is like the blood—the chemistry."

So saying, he goes over to the SEATED NUDE, MADEMOISELLE ROSE by Delacroix:

"What nobility! Things like this, after all, are greater than Courbet."

There are Corots all around us. Chagall comes to a halt before LA TRINITÀ DEI MONTI:

"Ah! What an artist! There, that is France. It leaves one speechless. There is a god. He transcends everything. It looks like nothing. . . . That blondness, that gray, that is France. . . . What were the Impressionists trying to do, after him? He already did everything. A real painter. He has the chemistry. He is a prince. He can do anything. He is a Mozart."

Which does not prevent him from appreciating THE PLASTER KILN, by Géricault:

"Terrific! The first Vlaminck."

In fact, Chagall's hesitations are never negative.

When he prefers a certain painter to another, it is less to take from the latter than to give to the former. For instance, he vacillates between Delacroix and Courbet. Now he is before ARAB HORSES FIGHTING by the former:

"It is painted like a Daumier. It is more distinguished than Courbet, one must admit."

Before THE ORPHAN GIRL, the comparison becomes clear:

"What intelligence, what nobility! Courbet was a great man, but his belly was too big."

And again, looking at THE TURKISH SLIPPERS:

"What distinction, what respect!"

A little later, however, when Courbet's HUNTED ROEBUCK LISTENING catches his eye, he says:

"Marvelous. What delightful tonality! Perhaps it is better than Delacroix."

With Chagall, hesitation is laudatory, ascensional. But he does not have to grope for contempt. A Puvis de Chavannes makes him grimace:

"This is Ingres' heritage."

Before canvases by Huet, Diaz and Decamps:

"Let's hurry, let's hurry!"

Raffet offers us his MARSHAL NEY, a perfect example of simple-minded imagery:

"This is Russian," I say.

"Polish, if you please."

And he adds:

"All pompiers are alike. . . . But perhaps the Russian ones are the most dreadful."

And here is our very own Russian, Meissonier, and his little pictures painted with a magnifying glass:

"Nightmares!"

"But after all, why?"

"A matter of chemistry. No talent. Like a singer with no voice. It is dreadful."

At times, I have trouble understanding him. He shakes his head, sighs, mutters: *"Nightmare!"* before a

Gustave Moreau, or an ironical *"the famous Decamps,"* *"the famous Rousseau."* With pauses for delight. Constable, HAMPSTEAD HEATH:

"That is Monet, there. I'm not mentioning Pissarro, because he is nothing."

Or Daumier, THEATER SCENE:

"Admirable! What is the secret of his greatness?"

Surprises, such as his reaction to STILL LIFE WITH WHITE PITCHER by Monticelli:

"One feels like stealing it. What an artist!"

Or his indulgence toward Millet and his RECLINING NUDE:

"He is not pompier. *He has good qualities, he has* Stimmung. *But it is finished, like Maeterlinck, like Levitan. It no longer touches one. Corot, yes."*

His HAYDÉE:

"The breasts are sagging, but the painting rises. What a genius one has to be! A little scumble. It looks like nothing at all. . . . That is what is lacking in Russia, in Germany: they always dot their i's. . . .

"My God."

Chagall has just caught sight of Watteau's THE EMBARKATION FOR CYTHERA:

"The grandeur, the concept, the madness of that thing!"

Of a JUDGMENT OF PARIS, he says: *"Cézanne did things like that."* And of the neighboring Pater: *"I cannot stand that."* Boucher, Lancret, Fragonard, he does not even look at. It is the GILLES that attracts him:

"That surpasses everybody. That comes close to Rembrandt. I would give all of Corot for that pair of pants. It sings and it weeps, like Cimabue. Corot has the song but not the tears. What one feels in GILLES *is not the feeling of death, but of the end of life."*

At a stroke, Watteau defines the limits of French painting by transcending it. Next comes a series of Chardin still-lifes, of which THE RAY:

Marc Chagall: À LA RUSSIE, AUX ÎNES ET AUX AUTRES

Antoine Watteau: GILLES

"The great French school comes from there. Scientific art . . . To end with Derain. I say: congratulations, hats off. But moved? No."

Thus, there exists another chemistry or, if you like, another aspect of the chemistry. The first allows us to enter into the historic, the visible; the second leads us out of it or, at least, orients the work toward a beyond-the-visible, a place common to all transcendent art:

"The great chemistry is the same, always and everywhere," Chagall says before a Fayum portrait. *"This Fayum portrait and a Corot are the same thing."*

The "great chemistry" is that by which we rejoin the community of nature, the "little chemistry" being that by which we rejoin the human community:

"The only pleasure I have: when the chemistry I produce in my canvases approaches the chemistry of nature. Like Monet, or the old Titian. . . . But one must live through one's times to reach that point."

For Chagall also, chemistry today is, above all, a matter of color. It is color that digs a tunnel to the untemporal in the canvas. Color depth: *"The color must be penetrating, as when one walks on a thick carpet,"* he wrote some time ago.

"I didn't even show my paintings to my friend Cendrars. I always used to think: we don't have many friends on earth; only our wife, because she has nothing against us. As a boy, I showed my paintings to my mother. She thought that I had talent but that painting was too difficult. She wanted me to become a photographer. As for my father, he was in another world. . . ."

A rather unusual circumstance explains this remark: on our way out of the Louvre, we are going through the Mollien Gallery, where Chagall is being exhibited at this very moment. A terrifying ordeal, dreamed of—not without fear—by Cézanne, Matisse, Picasso, and so many others. I can vouch for the fact that Chagall talks about himself without indulgence:

"No draftsmanship. It could have been done with the fingers. The color, that is what gives it the Geist. No stylization, no maestria, no pursuit of gesture. The weakness: the way an old man is young. Ordinary. The more ordinary Delacroix or Corot are, the more they are geniuses. What really counts? Who can say? It is like a child asleep in a bed. The color? You buy it in a store. The themes? I borrowed from the Bible because it is a first-rate book. There is no science in me. You must not draw well. Leave your talent alone. Ingres draws well, and it is a nightmare. I could have done my lines differently, on the right instead of the left, up high instead of down low, it would have been the same thing. To the excited, I feel like saying: calm yourselves, be like Corot, be ordinary! Stanislavski used to say to his actors: calm yourselves, drop your shoulders, then we will be able to see your true colors. It is like pissing: if it does not come, it is because you are sick. I do not like the grand gesture. In THE THIRD-CLASS COMPARTMENT Daumier has no gestures: fortunately, he did not know it."

Marie-Hélène Vieira da Silva

Is it that look which, when it falls on me, seems to come back from so far away? That hushed voice, singsong, slow, which loses itself so easily in silence? The moment they fall beneath my pen, verbs slip into the past tense, sentences seem to acquire the thin, melodious transparency of memories, and I almost feel constrained to begin this account of a visit to the Louvre with Vieira da Silva with the "Once upon a time" of fairy tales. I would not, moreover, have to exaggerate very much:

"When I was five years old, I used to visit English museums quite often with my aunt. She had a marvelous way of talking to children."

A little girl in a fairy tale in which aunts (rather witchlike) would take their nieces for walks not through enchanted castles but through the National Gallery, and in which the pictures in the mysterious magic books would be reproductions of paintings.

"At home, we had a big library full of art books. My mother was very quiet, a dreamer. I had no friends: so I became attached to these books. When I wanted to hear some noise, I would have to make it myself."

Translate: she would make music. At a very early age, she spun a web of analogies between sights and sounds that was never broken:

"At times, I am not quite sure whether I am hearing or seeing."

She adds:

"When I arrived in France, my education was more advanced in music than in art. At nineteen, I knew Debussy very well, but I had not gotten past the Post-Impressionists."

She arrived in 1928 and enrolled at the Grande-Chaumière. *"I was looking for contacts, I needed a place to work."* Earlier, in Portugal, she had taken courses at the Beaux-Arts School. The figure, anatomy . . .

"I liked the bones, not the nerves or muscles."

She discovered the Louvre:

"The first time, I suffered a great deal. I felt lost. It was too hard for me to grasp the content of the old masters. I was unable to overcome the distance between them and us. I was ashamed, I had qualms about copying them, because of that distance."

This is the peculiarly modern experience of rupture. We have acquired the ability to embrace history, it seems, only to be made to recognize its lack of homogeneity. Vieira possesses this sense to a very high degree. She remarks:

"In the Middle Ages, they made very skinny legs, and then suddenly along came Rubens, who made enormous legs."

And, finding ourselves in the Venetian gallery:

"If an inhabitant of another planet had come to earth in the year 1400 and then returned one century later, he would surely have thought that it had been occupied by a different race between his two trips."

The present day, noting the rupture, has usually

turned its back upon that past from which an abyss separates it. Not so Vieira da Silva. As she was first plunging into the fray, in 1929, she was also coming to the Louvre once a week. Even today, she experiences these visits, admittedly more rare, *as a need.*

Vieira is neither discouraged nor liberated by the abyss that separates us from the works in the Louvre. But she is attracted by them. Not that she finds them close to her; on the contrary, she loves them in their remoteness, for their remoteness. For this distance is the very indication of the time elapsed, the dimension of the memory—one might almost say: the present face of the past.

"These things are no longer ours. They give us the pleasure of escapism."

Long galleries of the Louvre, corridors of memory, the tunnels of personal and cultural time blend, or rather complement each other, to define an ideal place, remote, which is, for Vieira da Silva, at least so I imagine, the seed of life, the infancy of her art, as the lines of perspective allow us to go back to that privileged point which gives birth to them:

"I paint places, but places seen from very far away."

Among other birdlike characteristics, she has piercing eyesight:

"When you see from afar, you see things which are not very clear. That is what I paint from close up."

Perspectives: now we are at the heart of Vieira da Silva's work. They lead to the most precious things, they are Ariadne's thread to the labyrinth of life. Everything that tangles it or interrupts it must be cut through, pierced: the bones are what count, not the muscles or nerves. Speaking about people in the street, she wrote one day: "I think about the invisible strings that pull them. They do not have the right to stop. I no longer see them; I try to see the mechanism that

moves them. It seems to me that perhaps that might be a little like what I am trying to paint." She delights in passageways, in well-arranged networks:

"When I arrived in Paris, I was enchanted by the Métro, by the organization of the Métro. It is like a fairy tale. The doors that open and close when and how they should, and the way you infallibly find the right route . . ."

The fairy tale, for her, is not about the people, the things or events along the path, but the path itself which allows us to encounter them, each in its own time. The child listening to a story being told to him by a kindly person bending over his bed reacts in just the same way. He follows the tale less than the spell-binding voice, the true thread of the story. What does it matter what it tells, provided it keeps going and that in its wake he reaches that place beyond the horizon that he would know for sure was happiness if, each time, he did not fall asleep just before reaching it.

The tragedy, then, would be the interruption, the broken thread, the blocked perspective. One of the very first canvases in which Vieira found her style is named THE STUDIO: a room which a curve suggestive of some toy train consecrates to childhood. The room is bare and all its lines aspire to flight, to convergence on an ideal point to which the wall in the back brutally bars access. In de Chirico's public squares, Van Gogh's CAFÉ WITH BILLIARD TABLE, Tintoretto's ABDUCTION OF THE BODY OF SAINT MARK, this dizzying sweep toward the infinite creates a tragic effect: here, on the contrary, the drama results from the intercepted escape.

Freedom: getting beyond the wall. Vieira says:

"What meant the most to me in the Louvre is no longer here. I remember . . . I walked around, I wandered, searching for the key to all this, the answer to all this painting which baffled me, tortured me. And then I found it. Way up high, at the other end of the Louvre, as if it were the end of something, there was a little room containing the Impressionists, Cézanne. On the back wall, a LANDSCAPE, *the large* STILL-LIFE WITH ORANGES *and, between them,* THE CARD-PLAYERS. *Those two little old men who never stopped shuffling the cards, playing . . . That was the key to getting behind the seemingly impassable wall."*

She has the knack, bestowed upon Alice by Lewis Carroll: mirrors do not reflect her image. A rare capacity for vertigo, which is to the body what perspective is to the mind. Later, going back down the great staircase, she would grip the railing:

"I have acrophobia. At Saint Peter's, in Rome, I felt myself drawn up toward the dome. And yet, it is very ugly. But I adored Bernini's colonnade. I could have gone on forever walking between the columns."

What in others is expanse, interval, with her becomes corridor. The essential of a story is its thread. Vieira narrates the art of narration:

"My paintings are, above all, organizations."

In the Métro, she must prefer the ride to the station. She suffers from anything that is stopped. Ideas, for example:

"When I was young, people with set ideas always pained me. I like them to hesitate, to see the pros and cons, to change their minds. I have heard that the earth might capsize under the weight of the glaciers. At times, I think that could also happen under the accumulation of ideas."

She has, on her forehead, the pained line of people who are consumed by scruples. Of CHRIST AND THE SAMARITAN WOMAN by Rembrandt:

"I used to look at it for whole Sundays on end. Not because I liked it, but because I thought it was the best picture for me to study, that it would teach me something. And indeed, the next day, I would seem to draw a little better. All the weight of that light, a light which weighs heavily, like gold. Arpad, who has eyes like a cat, told me that he had gone to the Louvre on a very dark day. Only one painting had been visible: LA SAMARITAINE."

But later, as we pass the Poussins, condemned to semi-darkness no matter what the weather, she points to APOLLO AND DAPHNE:

"That, too, is very beautiful in the dark, but it is not heavy like Rembrandt, it is light. And yet they are both beautiful. That is why one cannot talk about painting."

After a long silence she adds:

"Klee wrote a book in which he defined Expressionism, Impressionism. . . . But Monet's FOURTEENTH OF JULY *has nothing to do with all that. . . . And that is what he forced his students to swallow."*

She likes Signorelli a lot:

"He talks very little."

Before THE PIPE by Chardin:

"It is so humble. The rest of them throw their still-lifes at you. One does not feel like eating the Chardins. The others, yes."

"But why?"

"To get rid of them."

If they are too brilliant, pearls make one forget the thread they are strung on. Vieira shrinks before the clashing cymbals of color. Painting in itself is already an excess.

"We stopped one day, my husband and myself, at a château on the Loire which had been converted to an inn. In the dining room, beneath some mediocre portraits, some very dreary, very gray people, retired, no doubt, were dining in silence. But the portraits were talking up a storm! The living no longer existed."

She has a cult for Corot, because his painting does not interfere with living. The great Baroque symphony —Titian, Veronese—is not close to her heart. She says:

"I am not attracted to violent colors. . . . That gray, it's exquisite!" she exclaims about BALDASSARE CASTIGLIONE. And about Mantegna's CALVARY:

"For me, there is almost too much color in it." Silence. *"Pliny the Younger complained that the Oriental influence caused too much color in the Roman mosaics."* Silence. *"When you paint gray, you have all the colors."*

Finally, after standing for a long time before Mantegna's SAINT SEBASTIAN:

"This is my painting. I cannot imagine the Louvre

*without it. Those gradations of gray in the volume of
the bodies . . . That very sharp drawing. The archer
is a Roman portrait. The tense, sustained, sharp drawing. Look at the arrows, how they are made. A great
strength that conceals itself. One cannot be harder and
quieter than that arrow. A pianist needs great strength
to play without making noise. Bach's suites for violin
and violincello seem to me to be the loudest possible
sound—louder than a large orchestra."*

Pallid, decomposed, the portrait of Chopin by Delacroix:

*"One smells the odor of the cemetery. Pianists rarely
play Chopin as Delacroix painted him."*

She contemplates Watteau's LA FINETTE for a long
time, in which lingers a trace of guitar music, and informs me that as a child she had torn out of *Illustration*
a drawing of a woman seen from the back, hanging a
painting, and had pinned it up over her bed.

*"Watteau's drawing is as powerful as Rembrandt's.
. . . What I love about painting is its musical side."*

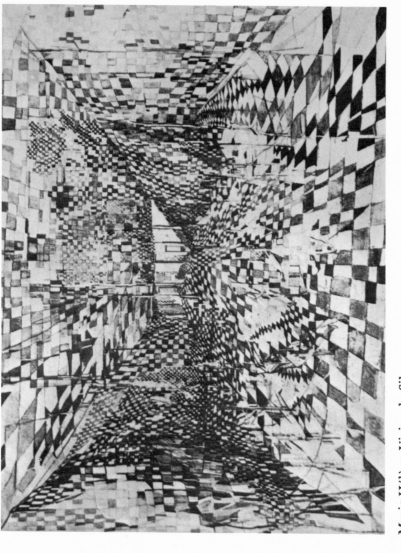

Marie-Hélène Vieira da Silva: LE CIRQUE

Andrea Mantegna: THE MARTYRDOM OF SAINT SEBASTIAN

So incantatory is her voice that it is only later, in reading through the words I copied down, that I can really hear their content.

THE BURIAL AT ORNANS:

"It was one of the passions of my youth. I had a passion for burials. In this room, it is Courbet who matters. What a black! And he has that sad quality of the nineteenth century: a sullen, rebellious, violent and well-fed society. The choir boys make me think of those portraits of dead Mexican children, painted standing up, very straight, as if they were living."

On that *absolute moment* that is the portrait of Chopin:

"One smells the odor of the cemetery, that is what I love about Romanticism."

And Zurbarán's BURIAL:

"Those people in monasteries, who led such austere lives. I am not a believer, but for me that would have been paradise, that cloistered, concentrated life."

A taste for the funereal, for the austere through which the will to convergence manifests itself. Vieira's THE STUDIO, already mentioned, in which the lines of perspective recede all the more clearly because the room is bare—is it not a monk's cell? In all of Vieira's canvases, there is this interior point toward which the marquetry of the surface is drawn. Tintoretto's SELF-PORTRAIT:

"He is looking inward. Rembrandt's SELF-PORTRAIT, in the Frick collection, is looking out. When I first saw it, I said to myself: 'I know the man who has those eyes, it's Picasso!' "

Surely, that voracious sort of look is not what she most likes to encounter. Before PARADISE by Poussin, painted a little awkwardly because of the tremor in his aging hand, and almost naïve because of its literal erudition:

"One thinks of Bauchant. Deep down, they were alike. In spite of Italy, Poussin has something of the old

French stained-glass artists: luminous colors on a dark background . . . Painting is very consoling. One can paint with a tremor, or almost blind. One's physical condition does not matter, almost."

She does not really like works in which the physical plays too great a role. Before the erotic meat display of La Pompadour's painter, Boucher, she recounts, with malicious glee, the story of a couple she saw one day at the Flea Market, in an art dealer's stall: "Have you any Bouchers?" they asked him with such insistence that the dealer in turn inquired why. "Because we are *bouchers"* (butchers).

Before the large full-length portrait of MADAME HARTMAN by Renoir:

"I am on my knees before this picture, but one cannot like it. It is like a blown-up balloon, soft, flabby, stupid. The fatness of these women gives me the impression of illness rather than of health. In everything he painted, there is a sensation almost of rottenness. But what miraculous painting: that blue with that black . . . Even the armchair has a lunar quality."

The voice is soft, distant. But beware! Her distances are not empty. Her softness is the plume that feathers the arrow: its point is sharp, at times cruelly accurate. Before the PORTRAIT OF CHERUBINI by Ingres:

"It is grotesquely ridiculous, and yet there are some very pretty things in it. The streaks on the left, for example; they remind me of Léger. I always found a resemblance between Ingres and Léger. Léger used very bright colors, but separated them with grays, whites and blacks."

She considers the old composer, painted in a very academic style, who has his hand up to his ear to capture the sounds the muse breathes to him:

"You might think he was listening to his agent at the Bourse telling him the market prices had fallen."

* * *

The voice is the voice of the aunt who speaks so marvelously to children, but the eye is the eye of a bird of prey, of a painter:

"*Constable, Bonington, reach us through the sky. Goya, through the earth.*"

By what is only seemingly a contradiction, she is at once elusive and perspicacious. For perspicacity helps see through and thus bring down the walls opposing the dizzy, delicious flight of lines, perspective.

"*One day, right after the war, Wols asked me: 'Tell me, I like what you're doing a lot, but why are you doing perspective?' I answered that I knew it wasn't done in modern art, but that I had to do it anyway.*"

To reconstruct perspective, she uses the very elements that Cubism—the dominant influence at the time she began to paint—had invented to abolish it. Cubism had split objects into slices as thin as playing cards, then had spread them out, thus forcing the forms into a frontality and an absolute submission to the design. Vieira, like Cézanne's CARD-PLAYERS, picks up the cards again and reconstitutes the deck. That is not just a simple metaphor: the cards, along with the checkerboard squares, the books on the shelves of a library, the keys on a keyboard, are among the materials Vieira is fond of using to construct her perspectives. The repetition of a simple, easily recognizable unit creates rows, rearranges simultaneities in sequence. The multiplication of a meaningless little square, seen up close, makes us lose ourselves in it, overcomes us with vertigo, and vertigo has its roots beyond the horizon:

"I love the long, blue faïence corridors in Portugal; the white tiles of the Métro, in Paris. I really loved the Bonnards exhibited around 1928 at Georges Petit's: tables with tablecloths with little red, yellow and pink checks."

But while Bonnard used those checks to rectify the space in a canvas and give the color a formal, over-all support, Vieira uses them in the manner of the Flemish and Italian primitives who turned to paving stones, roof tiles, to deepen the still shallow space inherited from Byzantium and the Romanesque-period.

I used the word "space" in the sense traditionally accepted since the Renaissance: in the sense of fictitious three-dimensionality. Our day has given it another meaning: that of actual expanse. Bonnard's tablecloths no longer recede; they constitute a frontal surface. In truth, the history of modern painting could be read as the progressive flattening of that imaginary depth created by the vanishing point. Thus it is the very course of time that Vieira turns back in returning down the path of perspective. And yet, she says:

"One cannot go backwards."

Delicate, elegant, airy perspective, like Mantegna's arrow, is also an instrument of death. The tragic sense in WAR, painted by Vieira during the dark years, flows from a double negative. The men are mowed down, lying in sharp receding lines, shuffled and thrown like the cards in a game all the more cruel in that it also subverts the artist's taste, making perspective appear infernal, when she would have loved, along with the men of the Renaissance, to regard it as divine.

The line which the bird believes is only the carefree line of its flight is the bar of a cage: the bird dashes itself against it. The *élan* loses itself in an unreal distance, the color bleeds here, on the surface. The wound inflicted by the impossible flight thus stains the walls of the cell with the colors of life. Accidents, but ones which give Vieira's work the character of presence.

"Accidents? Of course: my organization is not as perfect as the Métro's. When I succeed in making a perspective without accidents and without being photographic, then I will be happy."

The accident, in her case, is the magnetic attraction of painting in its present state, which is, whether Vieira likes it or not, frontality, acceptance of the surface. Once the arrow flying toward the focal point feels this attraction, its trajectory inflects, swerves. In the grid of the perspective, waverings and knots appear. And this disturbance, this opacity, this angry trampling attest to an equal fidelity to nostalgia as to realism, designating the exact point between the material surface and the ideal vanishing point where the conflict which defines Vieira da Silva's work knots and unknots itself.

For, strangely, it does unknot itself. The wound inflicted in the distance bleeds quite close to us. She declares:

"I want to paint what is not there as if it were there."

She succeeds in the fashion of certain Renaissance artists who reconciled two antinomic worlds by submitting them both to the same harmonic law: it is to musical proportion that Palladio, for example, en-

trusts the problem of conciliating the contrasting and divergent characters of the modern villa-farm and the ancient temple, as opera harmonizes the voices of two singers who, on the stage, cannot see each other by subjecting them both to a single score.

The role of music, with Vieira, is not a simple affair of motifs, of equivalences. The painting must be music in order for it to surmount the contradiction. For alone among the arts this one is at once sequence (perspective) and presence (frontality). The succession of precise notes melds into a totality.

Music is an unfolding, a flight of sounds, but the will of the composer, at each instant, foresees, recalls, weaving into the fabric of time another web which denies time: it begins without beginning, ends without end. It simultaneously goes through the looking glass and looks at itself in its surface. To pass through the surface while at the same time registering on it, that is precisely the problem the Portuguese artist sets herself. No doubt she would have judged it insoluble had it not been for her special way, as a child, of making noise: music.

We went the length of monotonous corridors full of sarcophagi and copies of antiquities, enough to discourage the best of good wills, and then came out among these paintings so remote from us, so remote from one another. Then I felt that perplexity arise again in Vieira da Silva, that anguished tension she had experienced during her first visit to the Louvre.

But now the anguish has given way to fervor. She finally realizes this:

"I associate the Louvre with Purcell's 'Ode to Saint Cecilia.' It begins with an overture without voices, noble, monotonous. Then, little by little, the voices come in, and it ends in variety, in exaltation."

Sam Francis

We are standing before a sun-drenched twilight scene by Claude Lorrain. Sam Francis says:

"The reactions of Americans can be told by their attitudes toward hair. Hair is organic. Hair is nature. Those who wear it short are Samsons shorn by the establishment. In America, everybody is either on the side of the machine or on the side of nature."

He says this in a quiet, composed voice, as if he were speaking to me about the relationships between Lorrain and Turner. Strange and yet believable: something which would be familiar elsewhere, if we knew the customs of the country. And I suddenly remember these lines from Saint-John Perse's _Anabasis:_ "Stranger. Who passed. Here to my liking comes news of far provinces."*

A stranger, that is what he was among us around 1949 or 1950, when several of us, writers and painters, come from the Old and the New Worlds, would converge, as at some secret order, on a _café-tabac_ on the

* Saint-John Perse, _Anabasis,_ trans. by T. S. Eliot (New York: Harcourt Brace Jovanovich).

_175_

Rue du Dragon. We rarely discussed art. It was near this billiard table, however, that notions of artistic communion, of participation, became meaningful to us. The history of art should be written from places of this sort and the spirit that reigns in them, but historians are rarely clients of the Brasserie Andler or the Café Guerbois.

As intimately as he was of us, Sam Francis, even then, was different: present and yet unreal, like the white creature in Rembrandt's NIGHT WATCH who sleepwalks through the gathering of good citizens of Amsterdam. Everything that was system, program, rule was banned from our conversations, as it was from the painting then arising. The labels that people, all too quickly, tried to attach to it—tachism, action painting, *informel,* Lyrical Abstraction—wounded us, as the sight of young draftees forced into uniform. The work of those years (including Sam Francis') ? "Bursts of unpremeditated art." But he alone among us seemed to have come "from heaven or near it."

He literally had fallen from the sky. As a pilot, he had crashed in California during a training flight in 1943 and had spent long months in a hospital immobilized on his back. A box of paints had kept him from boredom. He started painting what he could see: the sky framed by the window, animated by the passing clouds, modulated by the light. At once he had found his subject matter, which was the absence of subject matter. He never went through the stage of learning to draw: to draw is to define, delimit, while for him the experience to be rendered was that of limitlessness, of infinity. He lived abstraction before painting it.

He began to paint it, starting in 1949, in Paris. In a narrow studio in the XVth arrondissement, canvases as deep and subtle as the sky were born. Other painting tended toward the scream, his toward silence. It did not explode: it imploded. Artists had always represented forms (figurative or not) in space: Sam Francis undertook to paint space itself. An apparently utopian enterprise: space only manifests itself between objects or around them. It was to dream of an absolute music, rising from no instrument at all.

By 1957, Sam Francis was able to travel. (Hadn't he always dreamed of having an airplane ticket that would enable him to fly any time, any where?) Paris, Berne, Tokyo, Los Angeles . . . He has studios everywhere in which he works, as if to emphasize that he is from nowhere, or, more exactly, that he is a citizen of what is the same everywhere: space. Here he is now passing through Paris, but was he ever anything but just passing through?

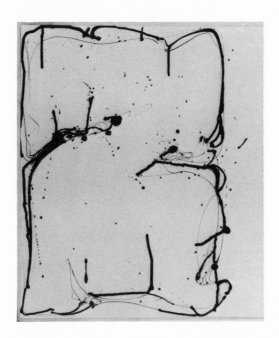

Twenty years have gone by since the meetings on the Rue du Dragon. Sam Francis' painting has renounced its modulations, has hardened. The color in it has frozen into sharp icicles. It has renounced its

"atmospheric beauties"—as Baudelaire remarked about
Boudin. Today it no longer offers an image of the sky,
a metaphor of the void: it is the void, or almost.

*"I have never been much of a museum man, you
know."*

I know. No more than he has learned to draw has
Francis looked at the works of the past. At the very
most the Monet of the NYMPHÉAS, less for the paintings than for the comportment of their author, for
that pantheistic attitude which led him to expand his
canvas in the mad hope of making the limited means
of painting adequate to express his experience of limitlessness. What is form for the artist who creates it becomes formula for the one who studies it.

*"The minute you define or regulate, you kill the
thing."*

Was Sam Francis still involved with painting? Com-
municating the infinite through the finite was possible
in periods when, through the intermediary of symbolic
language, a certain line, a certain color could stand for
it. But our time no longer offers systems for converting
the relative into the absolute. As a result, anyone who
would reveal an absolute is forced to do so in a literal
manner. If art can be defined as a divergence from the
literal, does Sam Francis' work still relate to what one
sees at the Louvre? In any case, he did not refuse to
go with me.

From where we are standing on the steps, not far
from the WINGED VICTORY, a dozen levels converge, in-
tercept each other, as in a Piranesi prison. On each,
the work of a different culture.

*"This museum just happened, that's why it's so
good. The stairway, the different levels, that great
room . . . It's like a Tower of Babel, an enormous
city. And that is how it should be. Today, we never
make room for the other levels of art."*

Plurality: remedy against the deadliness of rules. The museum consecrates hierarchies: it also topples them.

"Museums should be like the street. They should be open all the time. No mystique, no spotlighting. Nothing to say: this is a masterpiece. Things are there, that's all. A big place where things are, where you can notice them or not—that's my kind of museum."

Sam Francis' studio in Santa Monica: a vast warehouse of no particular character, open to every artist who wants to work there. Some, isolated, paint there, meditate, eat; others gather around a tape recorder, a guitar, a projector. Like a street, a covered square. *"A place for anybody to do what he wants,"* he had said to me as we were climbing the steps of the Louvre. I had been astonished by the association of ideas. It seems obvious to me, now that I have seen the studio. Like it, the museum is a large and welcoming enough

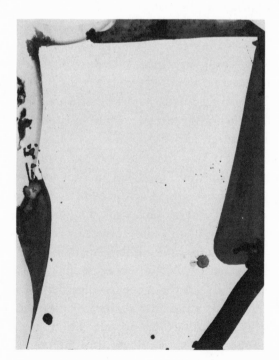

space to accommodate the most diverse voices.

We enter the Grande Galerie, where the crowd comes and goes.

"I love it. It's like the corsos in Italian cities."

From Christ down to the dog, there's room for everyone in Veronese's THE WEDDING FEAST AT CANA, the largest painting in the Louvre.

"I get a real feeling of gigantism here, because of the frame. Who would ever think of putting a frame like that around a painting that is in space?"

The first painting that attracts my companion's attention allows him, evidently unbeknownst to him, to get to the heart of the problem which, outside all references to the Museum or tradition, presents itself to him. The colossal scale: Sam Francis was one of the first Americans to recognize in the outsized the imprint, however approximate, of space and little by little to make it the subject matter of his work. Of course, the immensity of space had been represented many times (think of certain Rembrandt drawings as big as your hand) on a small surface or, as in THE WEDDING FEAST AT CANA, on an extensive one.

The new thing was to realize that a painted space, after it reached a certain size, could only have itself as a subject matter. To depict the sky on a canvas as large as a cigar box or a suitcase has a meaning: to paint it on a canvas which has in common with the real sky that it exceeds what the eye can encompass at a glance is a ridiculous pleonasm. To portray on such a scale people, a dog, a table covered with platters of food is no less impossible. Enlargement—scaling up— changes the nature of the enlarged image. Look at those old, overly blown-up engravings that adorn the walls of so many cafés: the texture of the black lines becomes distended, whites appear. But not just any white: the one that shows through in filigree is a pure absence, frightening, unbearable. It is the void which should not be seen. Perceived, it makes a spot, grows larger, filters through every chink. Space can only represent itself: it is invisible. That frame that made Sam Francis laugh, not without reason—does one frame the Pacific Ocean or the Gobi Desert?—has its usefulness. It reveals the invisible. It is the passer-by, the bus, the candlestick that transforms the pencil sharpener into the Eiffel Tower. It is the eye of the **needle that makes the camel.**

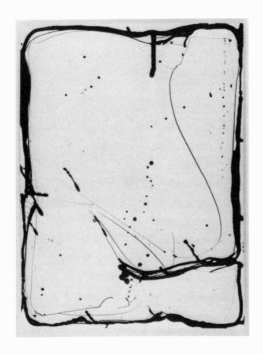

In the Grande Galerie, rehung a short while ago, the seventeenth- and eighteenth-century French school has replaced the Italian painting. We stop before Fragonard's CORRHESUS AND CALLIRHOE:

"Ludicrous, insensitive. No emotion. Everything that grows out of emotion is all right."

No reason to linger in Boucher's domain. I drag
Sam Francis along toward the Great Century. Le Nain's
A FAMILY OF PEASANTS IN AN INTERIOR:

*"This is the kind of painting that leaves me cold. No
air. You can't breathe."*

The property of space being not to have limits, a
precise outline or firm contours are just so many
wounds to it. So it is not surprising that Francis should
show himself to be hostile to Le Nain. What is surprising is that, turning away, he adds:

"My world is Poussin."

One of the great merits of the new arrangement is to
have finally accorded Poussin the space that for so long
had been so stingily meted out to him. Francis finds
THE TRIUMPH OF FLORA *"beautiful."* THE ADULTEROUS
WOMAN pleases him.

"Still, it seems fairly dry to me."

*"Not dry: hard. A mineral world. One is somehow
reminded of Piero della Francesca."*

He reacts instantly to the contradictions that tear at
THE RAPE OF THE SABINES: in the lower half of the canvas, the agitated men; in the upper half, the immobility of the architecture:

*"All the tugging and pulling against the absolute
stillness and solidity of the upper part of the painting."*

Once again, I note that a painter—this one has certainly never studied Poussin—at once grasps what the
historian has great difficulty extracting. One of the keys
to Poussin's work is the acceptance of—and resolving of
—extreme tensions. That is precisely what the SELF-
PORTRAIT before which we have stopped epitomizes:
the rational precision of the geometrical plan in it
clashes with the strange fiction of the woman's forehead studded with one eye. It all resolves itself, however:

*"Pretty solid man. Tremendous stability. Poussin is
always the same. No development, no ups and downs,*

no masterpieces. Great!"

Like drawing, breaks in the itinerary are wounds. Space is uninterrupted. The only thing compatible with it is that which merges with it, as light with sky:

"Poussin has 'lumière'. I just can't take painting that hasn't."

Turning around, we notice Georges de La Tour and the candlelight effects in his MARY MAGDALEN WITH A LAMP:

"It repels me."

Light is not synonymous with lighting. The latter is an armor plate that obstructs the painting a little further, because it is localized. And locality and space are contradictory. Light can signify space because it comes through windowpanes and slips between the bars of the forms. Nor is color necessarily local; it can merge with space like stain with a river whose course or flow one wishes to determine. Color: the visibility of space and its vehicle for slipping between objects, for spanning precipices, filtering through the most boring allegories, the most cantankerous forms, spilling beyond its time, beyond its frame. Where space is limited—and thus seems excluded—but color still admitted, space is present all the same. And I think of those Sam Francis canvases, not vast enough to be identified with space, and of the others, far too large to tolerate an enclosed image without ridicule (one thinks, for example, what a ham raised to the scale of the universe would be like) : their various fates entrusted to the intensity of a yellow, of a blue, which frees them from their borders. We are standing before Poussin's last painting, APOLLO AND DAPHNE:

"I never saw that blue before."

At different spots in the Louvre.
Fra Angelico, THE CORONATION OF THE VIRGIN:
"It reminds me of the hippies. It's psychedelic paint-

Sam Francis: ARCUEIL

Coptic art from Fayum, Egypt:
YOUNG GIRL WITH GOLDEN BREASTPLATE

ing. Sweet, candid, full of effects and sentimentality: 'We will be good!' "

A pause for thought:

"But the predella is fabulous. Much better than the upper part of the picture. So clear, so devoid of everything that mars the top. The top is flat and decorative, the bottom has depth. It eats into space like an acid."

Cimabue, THE VIRGIN WITH ANGELS:

"Those beautiful wings! Like space. You go right in. Like a landscape, or mountains, or clouds. Great."

Goya, LA MARQUESA DE LA SOLANA:

"Beautiful. It really relaxes one. Enormous room. All mineral and air."

The series, so badly hung, of portraits of the Fayum (*"I have always loved them"*). A woman's face:

"She looks like a monster; the scale is fabulous."

Another, this one of the YOUNG UNKNOWN ROMAN (inv. 3514):

"Beautiful. Like a cloud."

Still another, the PORTRAIT OF A YOUNG WOMAN:

"It has scale. It immediately makes me feel as if I were looking at a goddess. It is immense. That is what I mean by scale. . . . Scale is volume."

What attracts Sam Francis in every work, one notices, is space, which first fascinated him in his hospital bed. It would be more accurate to say: *beyond* every work. For in Poussin or Cimabue space is only glimpsed, a thread of light through half-closed doors, crumbling galleries. To grasp this thread, follow it to the total opening, all the way to freedom, that is the objective.

Sam Francis' objective, also the objective of painting during the course of its modern history, which reads, in fact, like an effort at disencumberment. Art—what we recognize as art—survives the diverse values that successive epochs and individuals identify with it because it consists of something else. Something which remains undefined, or at least is only defined negatively, as certain mystics define God: the space of painting is not synonymous with the power of the gods it represents, nor with the beauty of people and objects, nor with the truth of a certain compositional scheme, nor with the nobility of the materials, since men drove divinities from their paintings without destroying art, since the ellipse was used in it as profitably as the triangle, and acrylic as gold. Finally, it was proved that figuration itself was not indispensable.

The work of art is like a house in which there is one room that is not shown on any plan. One knows that it exists because light filters from it, brightening the adjoining rooms, the furniture, the people. No one has ever been inside it. Or, if someone has passed through, it was without realizing it. But after the fact, remembering that particular empty space, the so intimate and so impersonal effect it had on us, we become aware of it.

Space accessible to everyone because it belongs to no one: as a square, a public place, is a lung in the thick of a city. Only that can be shared which nobody possesses: liberty.

To give is to take away, when what one gives is a transfer of property: the named god who hid the divine from the painter will hide it from whoever looks at the painting. It is lighting substituted for light. On the other hand, to take away is to give, when the artist clears away whatever blocks access to the empty room. Sam Francis has posed himself the problem: how to give without giving oneself, without imposing what belongs to one alone and therefore cannot belong to another; or could only belong to someone else on the artist's conditions? He notices and loves in Poussin, Goya, Cimabue, a mineral, airy aspect: something made by the hand of man and yet in large part inhuman.

"Is that why you welcome artists into your foundation who might be described more or less as technicians: specialists in light or sound projection? You even seem to be turning to mechanics yourself: the use of cameras, phonographs, airplanes . . ."

"*I am not concerned with man-made inhumanity. Nor are the young people who work at my place. They are artisans—the last artisans left in the world—not technicians. They are not with the machine but against it. They try to destroy it. Space is natural. Artisans are related to nature.*"

Spontaneously, Sam Francis' eye breaks free from the borders of the painting thanks to a thread of light, a cloud, or, if there is nothing but a wall, by transforming that very wall into a cloud. He traverses obstacles, enters into the domain of dilation, of limitless expansion. The day after our visit to the Louvre, Sam Francis said to me:

"*I had a dream last night. Not easy to explain. I was in an architecture, a system, a language, articulated by light. There were different levels, like a city. There were moving shapes and shadows. One entered the shadows into a deep space. It was like liquid light.*"

Around 1947, that dream seemed about to become reality. The essential—the room beyond—by dint of successive eliminations was finally sighted, very close, about to appear. Perfect coincidence between an individual and history: that was precisely the moment when Francis began to paint. The evolution of art clamored, at that turning point, for an artist to be violently enough attracted by the void to push painting into it; but this artist, however great his desire and will, could not have crossed the threshold had it not been for that predisposition, that lessened resistance bordering on inducement, in painting itself.

So Sam Francis eliminated images: all shapes are human. Only stupid forms remained, for a time. Then, for the color of forms he substituted the form of colors, unreal because only a decipherable handwriting can actually be outlined, defined. "*Like a cloud, all mineral and air"*: the man must be abandoned at the threshold. Sticky tatters. Those large monochromatic canvases, so delicately shaded, these others, pulsing and fleecy, were still too reminiscent of clouds and the sky. A metaphor for space, as we saw, rather than space itself. Anthropomorphic, then, since metaphor is an exercise of the mind. It was to disappear, too.

At the limit, painting itself gave way before the space to which it had only been an approach. Its disappearance was the logical consequence of the kind of

negative theology which motivates its recent history. By 1960, everyone was grappling with this problem. Sam Francis was tempted to go all the way. Since painting must give way to space, the canvas from then on was to count less than the studio. He built large hangars, occupied warehouses, immense ballrooms. His canvases were packed into them, empty or not, but also artists of all sorts moved in—those who wanted to create something. *"A place for anybody to do what he wants."* Even THE WEDDING FEAST AT CANA could have been celebrated in them (by the way, sometimes considerable parties did take place). But why stop after such a good start? Why not use the sky itself, which formerly one simulated? Francis sent up balloons and kites, had a plane do sky-writing, tracing figures of smoke in the blue. The ex-pilot, at the end of his journey to the absolute, takes space literally.

But the essential, once reached, ceases to be that. Occupied by squatters, the public square can no longer be a place common to all. The value of the void was precisely its vacuity; that of the beyond, of the distance which preserved it from annexations. It is like those Delacroix paintings of which Baudelaire said that, seen from close up, they are a chaos of brushstrokes and that they only become meaningful from a distance. Space exists only at a distance. Freedom can be read only between the lines.

"White is the space between," Sam Francis said one day. Was this not a premonition that all those accessories—images, forms, compositional plans, etc.— which painting was struggling to eliminate were really necessary to it? That all the things which made it absurd—the canvas forever exterior to its subject matter, at odds with it—were exactly what permitted the essential to take root in it? Is that why the last paintings are as blank as a refusal, except for a thin fringe of color: the paint slipping off, sliding, bleeding at the edges of the glacier where it makes a last desperate effort to cling on?

Sam Francis continues to paint *because* painting is limited. The hardest thing for a mind that has mounted the camel of the absolute is to guide it to the eye of the needle. Sam Francis, returned from his celestial spheres, accompanies me to the Louvre, narrows down his visual field and says things so precise they seem to me to be the proof of those indefinable ones of which he claims to be the messenger. Here, THE RAY by Chardin:

"So wet, so emotional."

There, Watteau's GILLES:

"Great. You can see it is a young man's painting. No disappointments."

Alberto Giacometti

To the Louvre? Giacometti accepts out of politeness—the man keeps his promises—rather than pleasure. A horror of museums? On the contrary. *"I have just about the whole Louvre stored in my mind, room by room, painting by painting."* To achieve such command, he has made use of the method employed by Western painters since the Renaissance: *"I have copied a great deal . . . practically everything that has been done since the beginning of art."*

A place where you can see practically everything that has been done since the beginning of art: this is, after all, a fair definition of a museum. Giacometti visited the Louvre assiduously during his first years in Paris: *"Every Sunday."* His preferences?

"What was most immediate, newest: Chaldea, Fayum, Byzantium. What I love in the past is exactly what is most like what I see, my way of seeing things. Chaldean sculpture, for instance. And I prefer a thousand times Byzantine to Western painting."

He "gazed" at art, and drew it to sharpen his gaze. *"In trying to copy a thing, you see it better. I questioned each work in turn, intensely, at length."*

Gazing, questioning: Giacometti's way of proceeding is summarized by these two words. He says: *"copy in order to see better."* And if one asks him what art is, he replies: *"A means to see better."* One senses that he is prepared to reduce art, his own art, to this simple activity: representing as faithfully as possible something that is there. So simple, in fact, that it becomes impossible. *"Take the contour which runs from the ear to the chin. How can one get into the canvas, on an extent of three centimeters, a line which seems twenty centimeters long? It is humanly impossible."* The sense of this impossibility led him, toward 1923, to give up this conception of art—*"because it seemed absurd to run after something that was totally doomed from the outset, no?"* He ceased to question reality; and, for a number of years, sought to take inventory of whatever residual certitude it had deposited in his mind, abandoning to anonymity and to quasi abstraction those fragments which he was unable to reconstruct—as in some incomplete robot-portrait. But where ends memory, where begins imagination? Gradually, Giacometti's work drew closer to Surrealism, into which, toward 1930, it seemed to have merged altogether. For Surrealism offered an alternative: shut those eyes that set impossible tasks for you, replace the real by the imaginary, the visual by the visionary. During that period, Giacometti ceases going to the Louvre: he will return there only the day when he is again to be concerned with reality.

So everything will begin all over again—the same absurdity, the same impossibility. Except for one decisive difference: Giacometti has discovered in the meantime that the unlimited possibility of nonrepresentational art is even more frightening than the impossibility of representing reality. The visual smashes itself against the reefs of the external universe: the visionary, unhindered, projects an inner world on canvas screen or into malleable clay. Like a tyrant, the visionary generates emptiness around itself and brooks no contradiction. Like a tyrant, too, the visionary suffers from this emptiness, sensing that so much solitude will lead to its undoing. No longer having any object, art becomes its own object. This Giacometti finds unbearable: for him, art is not the end of a vision,

but a *"means of seeing,"* a school for looking. Indeed, I know of no artist who perceives the components of a painting or a sculpture as sharply; and one would swear that this sharpness is contagious. In the course of our walk through the Louvre, he had only to stop in front of a canvas and to scrutinize it for people to assemble and to do the same.

A school for looking: school is a gradual process. The dangerous thing about art, as Plato noted, is that the charm of the instruction provided threatens to keep us indefinitely tied to the school bench. Giacometti is of quite the same opinion.

"I used to see the world through the goggles of the

existing arts. I would go to the Louvre to see the paint-
ings and sculptures of the past, and I found them more
beautiful than reality. Today, when I go to the Louvre,
all these representations of the external world—and,
until fifty years ago, all painting, all sculpture were
direct representations of the external world, weren't
they?—strike me as partial, precarious. I ask myself
how the devil they could have seen it like that. And
what astonishes me, what really gets me, isn't the paint-
ings and sculptures any more, but the people who look
at them. Now I look only at the people who are look-
ing. They don't resemble at all—or almost not—the
representations that have been made of them. They
are so much more extraordinary that there have been
times when I almost found myself forced to run away.
. . . . Lately, I was looking at some Chaldean sculptures,

when I saw a woman leaning over one of them, looking at it. At once, the Chaldean sculpture became a rather crudely hewn stone roughly in the shape of a head, whereas the head that was looking at it became something dazzling, wondrous, completely unknown. I could look at nothing else but this person."

Reality alone is able to awaken the eye, to raise it from its solitary dream, its inner vision, and to compel it to the conscious act of seeing. For reality is the visible, and like jewels which lose their sparkle when they are not worn, the visible, it would seem, only comes to life in the beam of our gaze. Illusion, perhaps? This much is certain: the mystery of reality's otherness irresistibly incites us to question it. And here we are: questions, answers. Clumsy questions, obscure answers, but never mind: thanks to reality, a dialogue is established.

"All activity is really unconscious—except dialogue. The only thing of interest is a dialogue with somebody about something, no?"

Because dialogue preserves us from finalities, from solitude, from endless hoarding, from sleep. It is the readiness to take part in a game of exchange. Man's redeeming virtue, according to Giacometti, is that he is a creature capable of dialogue. If he himself detests sleep, it is because one is always alone in its folds. He likes places where people talk; he is given to contradict others (and himself) in order to keep the conversation alive. He goes to the museum as one goes to the café or to the forum: the works of art are partners in a discussion. A ceaseless motion, almost tangible, is initiated between him and them. He steps closer, steps away, charges in again with such animation that one could suspect that they are really replying to him. It is a dialogue with everything visible.

Such faith in the virtues of dialogue remind me of those modern economic theories which claim that the

health of an economy resides in exchange, in the uninterrupted flow of money: if the flow stops, if the
money accumulates, lethargy and (soon) the fatal
crisis ensue. Hence it is necessary—paradoxical as it
may seem—to engage in deficit spending. The loss en-
riches, activates. It is in this sense that Giacometti,
while considering that the act of representing reality is
doomed to failure, nevertheless regards it as useful, as
necessary. Thanks to it, art avoids becoming an object
and remains an instrument of exchange.

I expected Giacometti to lead me toward the sculptures of Sumer or the paintings of the Fayum. But, no.
A quick glance at the great Roman mosaic of THE
BATTLE OF THE AMAZONS, to point out the tragic character of the bleeding man, and he says: *"What I really
want most to see is Le Nain's* CART.*"* Is Giacometti repudiating his earlier enthusiasms? He has questioned
those works so much that they are now an integral part
of him, and this hampers the dialogue. One is reminded
of the two friends described by Nerval, who knew each
other so well that they guessed the slightest cause of
their slightest thoughts. Having nothing to say to each
other any more, they limited themselves to playing
dominoes.

As we walk up the stairs, I think of Giacometti's
situation in contemporary art: isolated by that will to
represent which links him to the art of the past. But
this fidelity, which in other times would have been
synonymous with facility, implies quite the opposite
today. It is as if the heir of a lengthy royal lineage felt
constrained by some inner necessity to assert his rights
to the throne at the very hour when nations trample
crowns (or, worse still, enshrine them in illustrated
magazines). An immense naïveté used to mask the
absurdity of the project of representing reality. Dürer,
Leonardo da Vinci, Seurat—prodigious, erudite
naïveté. Our century has destroyed this candid faith.

Abstraction is perhaps merely a form of caution, the natural consequence drawn from our awareness of the impossibility of representing the world.*

Giacometti fully shares this awareness. His undertaking is all the madder for it. Although disenchanted, he persists in accomplishing an act for which only naïve belief could give one enough courage.

"Are you really that isolated? Underneath the sur-

---

* Abstract painting of the "lyrical" or "action" variety has now, evidently, been deserted by younger generations of artists and pronounced dead by older generations of critics. It is worth noting, however, that, despite appearances, the recent brands of "realism" are still basically abstract. The world is not actively seen by them, but passively accepted, incorporated. One cannot speak of things seen, because the artist is not really *looking*, in the sense given to this word by Giacometti's practice and remarks.

face agitation of the subjects represented, doesn't the concern of painting remain constant through the ages? In the Poussin exhibition, held in these very rooms, were drawings that Mondrian would not have disclaimed. And they say that Kandinsky discovered the realm of abstraction by turning a landscape upside down. . . ."

"*That strikes me as excessive. One says that one remains 'in the tradition,' that one simply 'creates the structure of the painting without its subject'—as if there could be structure without subject. As if the subject were something banal and accessory superimposed on the painting! Take away the subject and you take away the painting.*"

"I see we are coming to the '*grandes machines*' of David, Gros and company. One step further, and we shall be with realism. You must be happy."

"*Realism is balderdash. . . . Those who came closest to the vision one has of things are those which art history calls the 'great styles.'* Yes, the works of the past which are generally judged most distant from it—I mean the 'stylish' arts: Chaldea, Egypt, Byzantium, Fayum, some Chinese things, some early Christian miniatures. But not at all what one calls realism! Egyptian painting, though people regard it as the most stylized, strikes me as realistic. Any one of us looks more like an Egyptian sculpture than like any other sculpture ever done. The same is true for the exotic arts, for the sculpture of Africa or Oceania. People like them because they consider them wholly invented and because they negate the external world, the banal view of reality. But they despise an academic Greco-Roman head be-*

---

* Giacometti here borrows the two basic terms in André Malraux's theory of art: "vision," i.e., ordinary perception, and "style," which implies the negation of ordinary perception in favor of arbitrary invention, subjective imagination, nonimitative creation.

*cause it is 'lifelike'—which, to them, is a contemptible
quality. I, on the other hand, like a sculpture from New
Guinea because I find it looks more like anybody—
you, me—than a Greco-Roman or a conventional head.
The most faithful 'vision' is that provided by 'style.'
Of course, nobody ever plans a style. For the Egyptians,
this would have been meaningless. They translated
their vision of reality as closely as possible. For them it
was a religious necessity. It was a matter of creating
doubles as near as possible to human beings. There
exists an ancient text, a kind of poem, which talks
about sculptures so true that they seem living and that
they are able to frighten those who see them. The
'style' in them is revealed to us by another vision. Egypt
has become a 'style' in our eyes because we see differently. But for them, who had only their own art to look
at, who knew only some Asian arts—only scantily at
that, and certainly were not interested in them—there
could only be one clear vision of the world: their own.
The same was true for prehistoric, Romanesque and
Polynesian artists. They had no choice. Only one valid
vision of things was available: their own. But today we
know all the possible visions, and we call these visions
'styles' once they are arrested in time and space."*

"If I follow you, 'style' is the consequence of sharpness and fidelity of vision?"

*"Exactly. I know that if I succeeded in making a
head somewhat as I see it, it would obligatorily look
'stylish' in the eyes of other people. Of course, I have
never yet succeeded. Still, there is something in my
sculpture that comes rather close. . . . The people
who look at my sculpture believe it is invented, no? But
what makes them look at it is the fact that it does
actually come close, fairly close, that it goes a little way
toward coming close to the way I see things."*

"When you speak of realism, you . . ."

"A realistic picture is a picture too unreal to become

'stylish.' The trouble with it is that it doesn't look like anything."

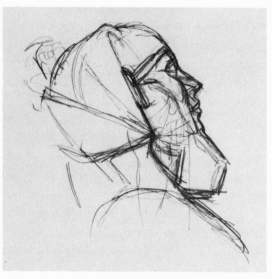

Perhaps this is why the gaze cast by Giacometti on the museum is so much more searching, more penetrating. We tend to think that all is done once we have recognized the style of a work. For Giacometti, on the other hand, style is only the symptom of the work's existence. To perceive its specific nature—and to detect what it is that makes it appear as the manifestation of an artistic style—one must go further, one must rediscover in the work that element which is vision and representation of truth. Giacometti is about to demonstrate the process for my benefit. We are at the top of the main staircase. On our right, Cimabue's VIRGIN WITH ANGELS.

"This is the painting I used to prefer, to find the truest. The brutes! They have put it on the staircase. They have expelled it from the Louvre."

We step closer.

"It is impossible to be truer to life. Here . . . it is those Roman excavations that changed Giotto. . . . Here: what could be truer, denser than the hands?

They are more real than Rembrandt's hands."

Something peculiar now occurs; I follow Giacometti's intense gaze and the Virgin's hands seem to begin to grow larger. Soon I see only them. They generate (and I am suddenly reminded of his sculptures that represent a foot, a leg, but so huge that one no longer thinks of the body to which they lead up) the void around them.

"What depth!"

We were looking for a thing's aspect: what we unexpectedly came upon was space's depth. It is the very dialectic of which Giacometti, in his own work, is rather the victim (albeit consenting) than the master. Part becomes bigger than whole; whole becomes smaller than the smallest part. The will to represent specific individuals gives birth to nearly anonymous figures; the need for dialogue reveals interminable, silent distances. These distances, however, are greeted enthusiastically by Giacometti. Without them, painting would be a mere decorative pastime. *"Today's abstract painters see everything in large format, in strong colors, in blotches without depth."*

The large format scatters our sight, the strong colors blind it, and the blotches drown the precision of identity, as the folds of a sumptuous garment blur the body's contours. Without precise, sharply drawn identity, no depth. It is the detail that differentiates a form, sets it off, separates it from others, generates around itself the void we call space. The infinities of space cannot be grasped in themselves (besides, as Pascal remarked, they are frightening). They must be baited by some tightly defined form. Reciprocally, the artist only gains access to space involuntarily. As a fisherman hunting for crabs is so preoccupied by his search that he pays no attention to the sea rising all around him until, raising his eyes, he sees himself isolated on a rock, the artist in quest of a precise truth finds himself, without realizing it until it has happened, assailed on all sides by depth. A depth so marvelous yet so dangerous that he must cling still more firmly to the appearance of things, thereby generating still more depth. . . . Thus the dialogue finds a kind of stability in perpetual motion.

"I see a tree like Mantegna or Van Eyck rather than like the Impressionists," he says in front of the SAINT SEBASTIAN. *They work in depth. The Impressionists see things as blotches. I used to be crazy about this picture—because of its colors: they are sparing, very sparing, and yet the result is the opposite of a grisaille."*

With a touch of melancholy, he adds:

"This is a truthful work. But it cannot be our own way toward truth. Mantegna has seen this head [the archer's] *the way I see heads. But I could never make it like that. The SAINT SEBASTIAN is like behind a curtain. One will never be able to lift it again. . . . What is staggering is that every discovery is at once irretrievably lost again."*

Perhaps "style" is merely "vision" after the curtain has fallen? At any rate, they are not contradictory. Before Leonardo's BACCHUS:

"At first, it looks real, and then it looks like a sign: at once dancing Buddha and swastika."

But that lesson is almost too dialectical. The heart of Giacometti's manner of proceeding is revealed by his next remark:

"And then, in contradiction with the figure, those flowers at the bottom. . . ." They are so delicate, so fragile, that you have to lean forward to notice them. *"This is truer, stranger than Dürer—a corner of China in Milano. . . . Those stalks: tall as trees. . . ."*

The East possessed superlatively the art (so close to Giacometti's dialectic) of making the immense surge from the delicate and of producing infinity by means of strict finiteness. The Balinese dancer moves knees bent,

almost crouching: when he raises himself, it is as if
he made a fantastic leap. The effect of upward fusing
is greater than that provoked by the Russian ballet
dancer, who never stops jumping. Before Goya's MAR-
QUESA DE LA SOLANA: *"What a marvel! It is made with
minimum means. It is as sparingly colored as Mantegna, and yet it is dazzling! Next to it, David and
Ingres seem horrible."*

It could be that Giacometti keeps up his steady com-
merce with culture because the sharpening of our gaze
through multiple confrontations teaches us to detect
ever more minute differences, to narrow down the scale
of aesthetic stimuli without weakening the intensity of
their effect. A scrawny tree on a square in an industrial
suburb impresses as sharply as the lushest jungle flora.
By overpopulating our awareness, culture renders us
attentive to the slightest variations. Cultural distance is
curiously alike to the distance for which Giacometti
looks in art. He waxes ecstatic before Corot's WOMAN
WITH THE PEARL. *"A funny kind of eye . . . faraway
. . . faraway. . . ."*

Like the figures that he paints and sculpts, Giacometti goes to the Louvre looking for interlocutors, but
finds solitude. But the very factor that makes contact
impossible stakes out the area of art: the space between,
depth. A painting of the past is as far—no more, no
less—as the tree or the model we try to represent. Before Tintoretto's SELF-PORTRAIT: *"You can't approach
it. It always remains at a distance, like reality. It is one
of the pictures I loved most when I first came to Paris.
It is the only one to come close to the Fayum, to Byzantium. It goes farther than Rembrandt (whereas
Cézanne goes elsewhere). It's the whole skull: the eye
but also the socket, the very structure of the head. And
it is done with nothing. Really, the finest head in the
Louvre."*

1954   Alberto Giacometti

Francisco Goya: LA MARQUESA DE LA SOLANA

Alberto Giacometti: NU DEBOUT

At last, our goal: Louis Le Nain's CART.

"After what we have just seen, it seems a bit dry, limited, a bit 'petit sujet.' "

But Giacometti's gaze insists and, already, judgment yields to dialogue; the perspective changes, becomes inverted.

"It starts improving right away, hein? One thinks of Chardin, of Vermeer. . . . It is dry like a whiplash. . . . What a marvelous figure! [the one in the left background]. *. . . The one at the right, in the foreground, seems more false. . . . No, not more false: it is seen differently.* [Under the gaze in search of the truth, the identity of things, they separate.] *The pigs, the group at the left, the landscape and the group at the right are painted in three different manners. It could be by three different painters. The woman with the pail is so beautiful that she makes a complete picture all by herself; you cannot even look at the figure next to her."* The silence that follows is like a correlative, in the mind of the gazer, of the depth that opens up between the parts of the picture; and then, by a further reversal, it is this depth which now will bind the disparate entities, as islands are bound by sea. *"Yet it all makes one composition."*

While Giacometti speaks, I see his own work defining itself in the filigree of Le Nain's picture, as if the disinterested ingenuousness of his gaze made the curtain transparent. What he tells me about his art he could never have told me without the mediation of another—without Le Nain's PEASANT FAMILY, before which we now stop. Instantly, the excruciating truthfulness of the details catches his attention and, in its beam, begin to grow: *"The bit of red in the wineglass gives the whole picture its color. Without it, the picture wouldn't exist. The candlestick on the table— grand as a monument on a Roman square."*

What I see is no longer a corner of a tablecloth but

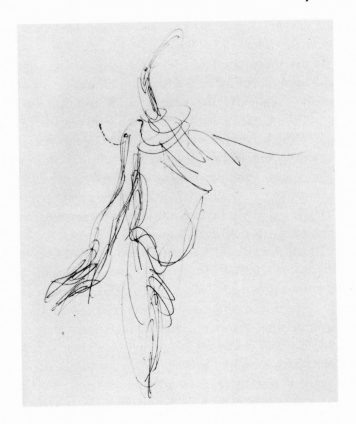

the Piazza Navona. But already he is saying: *"What sympathetic heads! . . . All those gazes do not gaze at us. That eye, what nostalgia!"*

"If people heard you now, wouldn't they think you've become a victim of anecdote? . . ."

"Ah, bien! Je m'en fous! . . . And the girl's eye: it has a Fourth Dynasty air. . . . And the old woman's head resembles the madwomen's heads by Géricault, heads by Rembrandt, by Corot, by Chardin. . . ."

Relation with reality and relation with art, dissimilar though they are, share the same pictorial presence.

"Here is a dark eye and here the Piazza Navona and here the Fourth Dynasty. Everything is equally true. The pitcher of wine placed on the table and the glass which the man holds vertically above it are things seen."

And yet they repeat the pattern of the superimposed figures in THE CART."

At the sharp point of the living gaze, artistic style and vision of reality are consubstantial; and this oneness does not make the present vision retrench itself behind the world of art but leads the works of the past back to the present of vision, embodied at this precise moment by one picture or another.

"It looks like everything . . . and like nothing. . . ."

Depth gradually invades the picture, absorbing the sharp forms that generated it.

"A soft depth . . . one enters into it as into music. How soft it is, how pleasant."

In the nocturnal musical depth of space, the faces that seemed so interesting a few minutes ago are nothing more now than nameless spheres, gently glowing. The images of reality are lamps that momentarily light space's dark chamber, in which all is soon isolated, devoured. Before the PEASANTS EATING: *"That fellow at the right—tired, lost, as if lost in the desert. Better to be lost."*

We cast a glance at the canvas hanging next to the PEASANTS EATING. It is by Louis' brother, Antoine Le Nain:

"Good, solid painting. Fine surfaces. But not those planets suspended in space, that music . . ."

And as the inexorable row of guards, formed at the approach of closing time, paces up the Grande Galerie, chasing us toward the exit, we throw a final glance at THE CART.

"When all is said and done, it is one of the paintings I like most, because of its color. Like pearl. It is— perhaps on account of the break made by the woodpile at the left?—like a little island adrift. At a distance, its color for me is of a. . . . It is the color of the countryside. Ah, la, la!"

Barnett Newman

"Great, romantic," he exclaims, looking up
at the Pavillon de l'Horloge. *"Real outdoor shapes.
Mansart's façades are like interior walls."*

It is the first time that I have heard one of my artist
companions comment on the Louvre as a building. In
part, this may be due to Barnett Newman's readiness
and ability to comment on practically anything, but
the main reason is that, as he tells me to my surprise,
it is the first time that he has seen the Louvre.

To be sure, there is always a beginning. Poverty, an
allergy to airplanes, to France, to a change of bars, may
account for a person's not setting foot in Paris before
he has turned sexagenarian. What is surprising, here,
is the fact that the man who confesses to this cultural
virginity looks like the quintessence of *Homo euro-
paeus*—I mean: like Emperor Franz Josef. The port-
liness, the jovial majesty, all the ingredients are there,
down to the Habsburg mustache and the monocle
dancing on the chest.

But when you belong to the generation of Pollock,
De Kooning and Kline, the world can regard you only
as a kind of fundamentalist, as the noble savage break-

ing upon the scene of art. Instant adjustments are therefore needed to reconcile visual observation with mental image. I tell myself that the Huron, after gobbling up Franz Josef, has donned his victim's uniform. Unless his motive was caution, not cannibalism: the complete outfit of the Old World *Kulturmensch*—whiskers, monocle, clothes—provides the noble savage with a protective disguise, just as the Huron, to be left in peace, pretends to be an oilman.

Wrong again. We are ascending the staircase leading to the WINGED VICTORY.

"I grew up on APOLLO *by Salomon Reinach,"* says the noble savage.

While I am trying to recover, he has reached the landing and is looking at the agitated sculpture.

"What are people talking about when they say it is classical? Futurism, that's what Hellenism is. The Hellenes must have been Italians, not Greeks. 'Hellene' means 'Jew,' I think."

Not having read Reinach, I cannot argue with this thesis. So we proceed to the Salon d'Apollon; above the Crown jewels, Delacroix's ceilings. Newman looks at a female nude, painted full back.

"It is always easier when you have a breast showing. It gives a new dimension. Gland instead of muscle."

Turning into the section of the Grande Galerie currently open, we come upon a potpourri of Italian Renaissance pictures. Newman's eye jumps from Carpaccio's LEGEND OF SAINT STEPHEN to the neon tube that zigzags along the ceiling. About the former: *"The feeling is Dutch."* About the latter: *"How do you like the shaped canvas?"* And as for Cima da Conegliano's VIRGIN AND CHILD: *"Calendar art, chromo. They needed it, because they had no movies."*

Neither Huron nor epigone, then, but both. The sense of hierarchy bred by knowledge coexists with the unordering, wide-eye-lens acceptance characteristic

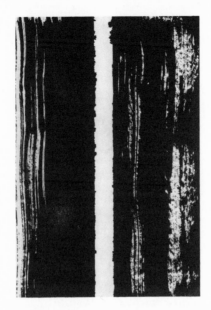

of first meetings. Actually, it is the satisfying of a desire long thwarted.

*"As a youth, I was always at the Museum. With Got-
tlieb, for four years, my weekend began at the Metropolitan. In 1925, it had two Cézannes on loan, a Monet
cathedral and* MADAME CHARPENTIER *by Renoir. When
the Museum of Modern Art opened, there wasn't a single painting I hadn't seen before, except* GUERNICA. *Only
it was by reproduction. The main work, in those years,
was to find the paintings. It took time. I used to blow
the whistle and all the tramps would come to Wilden-
stein. In those days, galleries didn't want students—
just potential customers. It was impossible to see modern art. Even, say, for Picasso, you would see 1925
Picassos in 1940. Maybe that was a good thing: today
a painting has become a cliché before it's painted."*

The figure who summarizes this traumatic denial
in Newman's eyes is Albert Barnes. As a youngster,
Newman had asked for permission to visit the Merion
treasure house. Barnes replied that to see his collection, he would have to join his art school. Roger Fry,

who was then lecturing there, thus earned his share of
Newman's lasting resentment.

Uccello's BATTLE:

*"Fantastic. Absolute totality. One image. I suppose
this is so because the light is even from corner to
corner. No spotlight—like Courbet. Monet, for in-
tance, was always spotlighting theatrically, except in his
late work. Hence his popularity."* He pauses. *"Physically, it is a modern painting, a flat painting. You grasp
the thing at once. What fantastic scale!"*

"By scale, you don't mean size?"

*"It is beyond the problem of size. It looks big. The
content and the form are inseparable: that's scale."*
He pauses again. *"It is a strictly symmetrical picture.
Hence its totality. It is like the symmetry of man. It
has no color: it is beyond color. It is not black, nor red.
The color is pure light—night light, perhaps, but
light. What bothers me is color as color, as material, as
local. In Poussin, a pink is a pink."*

THE BATTLE OF SAN ROMANO, by now, has become the
work of Barnett Newman. Cognition is recognition.
We stand before Mantegna's SAINT SEBASTIAN. He looks
at it rather casually, not to say disapprovingly. To break
the awkward silence, I tell him that Giacometti loved
this picture.

*"Saint Sebastian looks like Giacometti: he must
have identified himself with it."*

Obviously, Newman has not.

*"I am surprised, frankly. It is so heavily illustrative.
The way he coolly takes all those arrows. It is like
Magritte. Those arrows are purely symbolic. They are
not going through flesh, but wood. Yes, now I get the
painting. As soon as I got through the Hamlet image to
the Surrealism, I became interested. As soon as you
read a painting, you can accept its style, the way it is
painted."*

The reason for the change of tone, from casual to

passionate, one may readily surmise: somehow, at one time, Newman must have been involved with Surrealism. The reading is the meaning. One of Jean-Paul's stories tells about the village librarian too poor to buy new books; to complete his library he would, whenever he came across a favorable review in a learned journal, write the book himself, on the basis of its title. We are all like Jean-Paul's librarian. There is no true meaning. Historical reconstructions, in writing or on canvas as in stone, are an absurdity, because a work lives through presence: the author gone, the presence must needs be ours. Iconology is for epitaphs. It is not surprising that Professor Panofsky should have taken Newman to task for making a mistake in the Latin of one of his titles, and that Newman should have defended the error: life is a spelling mistake in the text of death. Just before coming to Paris, Newman had been to Dublin, where he took part in an exhibition. Part of the exhibition consisted of "Celtic" masterpieces, among them the Book of Kells.

"I looked at the illuminated initials on the opening page and let out a yell: they were my initials."

Needless to say, they weren't. In fact, they couldn't be, for they were the initials of *In principio verbum.* But for a few moments, the old painted manuscript was as actual as any work in the Whitney Annual. The convolutions of the Irish style had made the mistake possible, not only by distorting the alphabet, but in the sense that they gave the page its beauty, which, in turn, made Newman want to identify with it. Meaning is the viewer's business, but the incentive which makes him want to mean, which strikes through to the zone of awareness where his interest is awakened—that is the picture's prerogative.

Back to the staircase, by way of Botticelli's frescoes (*"It's really drawing, not painting"*) and the hand of the WINGED VICTORY (*"Without this hand, Giacometti*

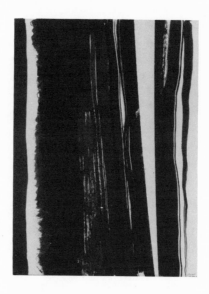

wouldn't have tried it, I suppose") . Facing us, Cimabue's VIRGIN:

"Terrific! This is not chromo. It's epic. I am struck by the uniformity of light, by the boldness. This artist is someone with a brain, not just a hand. He did not make the Virgin a simple girl, or a virgin, but a powerful person, a matriarch. She certainly doesn't look like a virgin—that's what makes the difference. It's an epic statement about the mother of God—not just any mother. Cimabue has the same boldness that made Grünewald give his Christ the syph. It is not only the heart that's at work here, but the mind. Not Vasarely's kind of intelligence. The insulting thing about these guys is that they feel they have a mortgage on the mind. And they reduce it to the table of logarithms."

Around us, the juggernauts of French neoclassicism. David's PORTRAIT OF MADAME RÉCAMIER:

"The long arm. Courbet, Cézanne use it too. It is out of MONA LISA. Those who put the mustache on the MONA LISA are not attacking it, or art, but Da Vinci. What irritates them is that this man with a half a dozen

*pictures has this great name in history, whereas they,
with their large œuvre, aren't sure."*

We wheel around: David's CORONATION OF NAPO-
LEON.

*"Talk about wide-screen! This was done before the
movies. I am not laughing at the guys who make movies
in pictures. I am glad that David painted this, otherwise the movie guys wouldn't have known what to do.
I am not joking about spectacle art: we just can't see
it with unspoiled, pre-movie eyes any more."*

An abrupt turn to the left takes us out of the
French circuit into the Salle des Etats, occupied—for
how much longer?—by the Venetians. At one end,
Veronese's jumbo WEDDING FEAST AT CANA; on the opposite wall, facing it as David did Goliath, the MONA
LISA. All around, the pictures are densely massed in
superimposed layers.

*"This is the way I like paintings hung. You pick out
your own. Otherwise, you get involved in boutique."*

Newman points to the figure of Christ, dead center
of the WEDDING FEAST AT CANA:

*"Here is a symmetrical painting that doesn't work.
It is so symmetrical that the symmetry overshadows
everything. . . . Also, it's fussy. It is really a small
painting, that's the trouble."*

Another Veronese, THE ROAD TO CALVARY, fares better:

"It is off-center, almost candid camera—like Degas."

The MONA LISA becomes an exercise in mechanical
physics:

*"Notice the way the arm, the shoulder swing. The
neck back, the shoulder forward, hence the lengthen-
ing of the arm. It is from her that Courbet and Cézanne
learned the trick of leading with the shoulder."*

So help me God, she is smiling. I hadn't seen her
do so in years. Talk physics, and sentiment will show;
talk sentiment, and you will see pullies and ropes.

He finds Tintoretto's SUSANNA AND THE ELDERS *"terrific."* Tintoretto's SELF-PORTRAIT reminds him of El Greco. *"Same look in the eyes, same depth. Very poignant painting."* Giorgione's COUNTRY CONCERT brings him to a halt. *"It's such a shock to see it. It isn't at all like the reproductions, it's human. Everybody talks about Giorgione's stylized image: I don't see it at all."* Titian—at least the Louvre's samples of his work—elicits mixed reactions. The PORTRAIT OF FRANCIS I: *"I'm not so crazy about it, it looks like a cut-out."* But he pauses at length before the VENUS, once in the possession of Cardinal Mazarin, whose long, lazily recumbent body does not quite succeed in binding the sections of this exceedingly wide picture.

"This is like three paintings added. Maybe only modern painting made multiple figure painting successful. That's why Uccello is so modern. In Matisse's DANCE *or in Picasso's* LES DEMOISELLES D'AVIGNON *or in Uccello's* BATTLE, *flatness reasserts a processional idea. They are really one figure with a reversal of heads. Giorgione's, Grünewald's pictures are successful because they are one-figure paintings. Picasso, Matisse catch the problem: flatness forces them to face the multiple-figure situation and to solve it. . . . The flatness of flat is something we solved."*

Back to the French school. After David, Ingres—but Ingres is missing, his paintings having been sent temporarily to his Centennial exhibition at the Petit-Palais. *"Let's go,"* says Newman, whom the morning at the Jeu de Paume (*"Manet is the greatest painter there"*) and the afternoon at the Louvre do not seem to have exhausted.

Greeting us, in the hallway, is the canvas that we should have seen across the room from David's CORONATION: the huge APOTHEOSIS OF HOMER.

"It makes that big Veronese look like a good paint-

ing. It is pure mirror symmetry. Ridiculous. He had to find a guy with a mustache for the right side of the picture because the other guy, on the left side, had one.

Next, one of Ingres' weirdest creations, THE CORONATION OF NAPOLEON; the Emperor is frozen, with all his regalia, in a frontal majesty halfway between Byzantine icon and Musée Grévin wax figure.

"Look at the bluish beard on the ivory face. The beard feels real, the flesh doesn't. It's like hair on a billiard ball. No question but that he had a sense of texture."

He looks at the carpet beneath the throne, which breaks into a sharp fold over a step.

"This, of course, is abstract: he is using language rather than bothering with the subject." Suddenly he laughs and points to the ivorine globes decorating the arms of the throne. *"And there they are, the billiard balls!"*

Intelligence is a pendulum. Newman has begun to swing. The portrait of Madame Rivière:

"It is abstract in the sense that it is area painting. Drawing is just an excuse to break up the painting into areas. There is nothing wrong with that; what is objectionable is the contouring. The guy couldn't draw. The coldness is all right: it is necessary to obtain the distribution of areas. He is a painter, not a draftsman. The quality of the painting is heroic, the quality of the drawing is bourgeois."

Around us, examples of Ingres' cult of antiquity.

"He couldn't have been foolish enough to think he could revive the Classics."

"He was a fanatic."

"That's not foolish. Delacroix, too, was a fanatic."

LA GRANDE ODALISQUE, so long-backed that critics of the time said she had three extra vertebrae.

"I am struck by the schematic quality. That guy was an abstract painter: the idea of handling the painting as a flat surface. He looked at the canvas more often than at the model. Kline, De Kooning—none of us would have existed without him. And he was involved with filling in areas; hence the absence of tactility. There is never a deep perspective: the pictures are planal, totally processional. This is not Classic, it's high Romance."

Romance: an unsuccessful pining for the Classic. It subsumes the tendencies of an epoch that dreamed of Homers and produced Ossians—OSSIAN'S DREAM is precisely one of the revelations of the exhibition—recaptured the power of the great ages only through historical evocations, the nostalgia of troubadours remembering the bards. (The *style troubadour* is, in fact, amply illustrated in the show by vignette-like canvases dealing with the lives of Raphael or Michelangelo, with Paolo and Francesca, Roger and Angelica.) The disparity between the objective and the means available, the epigone shoulders striving to carry the burden of a grand tradition too heavy for them, the tensions and original twists engendered—these are Mannerist traits characteristic not only of Ingres but of his time. Newman's remarks were born of pure visual observation, yet they are relevant to cultural history. He has demonstrated, as a viewer, what he asserts as an artist: that the visual and the mental form a continuum.

We are before the portrait of Madame de Senonnes, a symphony of muted browns:

"He is sort of sensuous, but his sensuousness is weird. Maybe he used to pride himself in how long he could hold back his orgasm. Passion, yes, but passion held. Corneille against Wagner. And no less passionate for being held. . . . The more you look at her, the lusher she looks."

Before us, the exception, the large bathing figure known as LA BAIGNEUSE VALPINÇON:

"The emotion here is tender. Look how relaxed the foot is. In this painting he has really relaxed the flesh. This is not a stone figure: only the drapery looks like stone. It is a terrific picture, passionate, soft—the opposite of the NAPOLEON. *No color. The real thing. I like him best when he moves toward monochrome."*

JUPITER AND THETIS. Classical dream veering to private obsession; the virile ideal of antiquity undergoing a change of sex; closer to Gustave Moreau than to Louis David:

"Thetis' foot! The toe is like an Arp. If only it didn't belong to this painting!"

If anything, Ingres was more absurd in his large-scale religious works than in his classical subjects. The protagonist of THE MARTYRDOM OF SAINT SYMPHORIEN, a declamatory figure no less devirilized than Ingres' mythological divinities, causes Newman to make a significant mistake:

"She ought to start singing her aria. It isn't Italian opera, though. Something of Brünnhilde about her."

(Yes, Ingres' nostalgia for antiquity: a Northerner's pining for the South.) *"The arms are too short. The man simply couldn't draw—no question about it. But he could paint like a whiz. He really thought he could draw, too."*

The dozens of arachnean pencil portraits on exhibition, freezing the edges and ridges of reality like fossilized ferns or early daguerreotypes, do not cause Newman to alter this judgment. Indeed, they confirm it.

"Drawing isn't a question of contouring, of anatomy. Ingres just had no sense of scale. He couldn't relate. But he didn't know it. No more than he realized that the epic was beyond him. Genre was his thing: a girl on a bed, etc. . . . He had a very false idea of his own talent. But that's legitimate. Maybe GUERNICA *will end up as a cartoon, yet there was passion behind it. . . . Maybe he read too much."*

On the opposite wall, the large, stereotyped VOW OF LOUIS XIII:

"A pure potboiler. But of course, in those days, the pot was a real pot."

Side by side, the portraits of Monsieur Leblanc and

of Madame Leblanc. His: *"The sense of wool."* Hers:
"The sense of silk." The feeling for texture is a logical
correlate of the abstract, planar quality of Ingres' painting, for textures are accentuations of surfaces. He adds:
*"They are not portraits, but genre. He was great in that.
He didn't hold back, there. Even though his brushstrokes don't show, it isn't cold. . . . Then you go on
to another canvas and he can't do it."*

Such breakdowns are accounted for by Ingres' phe-
nomenal misjudgment of his capacities: those of a min-
iaturist haunted by heroic formats and themes. As
Newman noted about the SAINT SYMPHORIEN, Ingres'
genius was contradicted (by the times, by his own
notion of what he was about). The contradictions were
probably part of the genius—the fanatic violence
fanned by the denials. At any rate, it is ironic that the
artist who aspired to resurrect the gods of mythology
should have painted the first effigy of that new creature
of unprecedented materialist opacity, the bourgeois:
Monsieur Bertin.

*"If only he had painted Napoleon like him! This
really is an emperor."*

Again, visual perception corroborates history, for I
am quite certain that Newman did not know that
Bertin, through his *Journal des Débats,* was a fore-
runner of the modern type of emperor, the press tycoon.

Another member of the new ruling class, in all her
frigid splendor: the Baroness de Rothschild. Newman
points to the scutcheon bearing the Rothschild coat of
arms painted in the upper right. *"It is like Whistler's
butterfly—a collage. Ingres is the only man, with Whistler, who can stamp on a symbol as if it were outside
the picture."*

Once more, the concrete, apparently limited observation has far-reaching implications. The quality of being
outside brings out the steely impermeability of Ingres'
surface: any sign must perforce appear stuck on, like a

price tag on a shield or lettering on a Cubist image. It explains, too, why Ingres was drawn, despite himself, to bourgeois models: their moral impermeability made them the living equivalents of physical textures—and therefore the adequate subject matter for an art that sought, albeit unconsciously, to assert the intransgressibility of the picture plane.

LA VIERGE À L'HOSTIE, a robot-reconstruction of a Raphael Madonna, and LA SOURCE, the saccharine icicle projected by means of countless illustrated calendars and dictionaries, from the artist's private obsessions into the collective unconscious.

"Potboilers, related to his ambition."

The self-portrait of 1858:

"Here the flesh is not idealized or petrified. He is living. . . . It looks like a professional portrait of a college president. It is the most academic painting in the show."

And the final work, in which the seventy-year-old master warms his chilled brush in the glow of a great sexual daydream—a harem crowded with nude, writhing, languid, passive object-women: *"It is like worms crawling."* Little suspecting that these were precisely the terms used by Paul Claudel to describe THE TURKISH BATH.

On the following day, we return to the Louvre, picking up where we left off: The French, still. Delacroix's WOMEN OF ALGIERS:

"Beautiful! It could have been done by the Impressionists. This man could draw." Pointing to one woman's naked foot, he adds: *"Drawing here doesn't only break up space, it exists as a line, as a thing."*

Next, THE DEATH OF SARDANAPALUS.

"In terms of scheme, it is interesting. The cut-out forms, the jumble. GUERNICA, *even Rauschenberg, is related to this. It is what in journalism we used to call*

'circus lay-out': make a mix-up of the page. It's like a three-ring circus. A lot of things going on at the same time. And yet there's more to it than just a lot of ingredients. The eggs, the salt, the butter are all needed, but the omelette is something else. . . . Terrific! What is interesting to me here is the spiral perspective, as against processional or vertical perspective. It is the first successful one I see. The picture really swings."

Facing it, is Delacroix's LA LIBERTÉ DE 1830.

"I find it stronger, more passionate than SARDANAPALUS. *I suppose I just don't like pink."*

Newman finds THE MASSACRE AT SCIO *"a bit cold and staged."* The spiky ENTRANCE OF THE CRUSADERS INTO CONSTANTINOPLE doesn't transport him either. *"He doesn't get what Uccello gets with his spears. You can cut out sections."* Gros's BATTLE OF EYLAU receives a nod of sympathy: *"The good thing about it is that the group makes a large form. He has some scale. But maybe it was just an accident. The horse looks wooden. . . . Sweet-looking face he gave his Napoleon."*

But all this is swept away the moment Newman becomes aware of Géricault's RAFT OF THE MEDUSA.

"Fantastic! The scale is marvelous. You feel the immensity of the event rather than the size of the canvas. Great! Wild painting! The space does engulf one. What's all the fuss Roger Fry made apropos of Cézanne's table tipping up about? This raft does it too. It has the kind of modern space you wouldn't expect with that kind of rhetoric. You can feel the surge of the water, the figures tumbling out toward us."

Géricault's OFFICIER DE CHASSEURS:

"Fry is nuts! The tumbling out belongs to Géricault. The horse is going away and yet coming forward. The guy is obviously interested in the problem of flat space (although everything in the picture is normally located)."

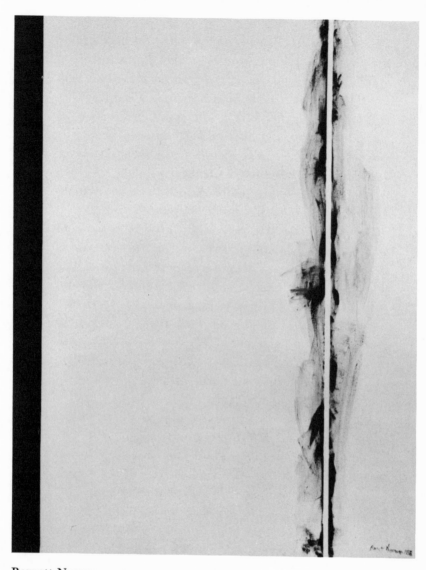

Barnett Newman: FIRST STATION OF THE CROSS

Eugène Delacroix: THE DEATH OF SARDANAPALUS

We have reached the other end of the gallery, Courbet's realm. The ROES' HIDEOUT, its green so deep as to seem black, the anecdote of stag-life swallowed by the silence of nature.

"This is the nearest thing to Uccello. There is nothing to scrutinize. You get it or you don't."

Courbet's STUDIO:

"I suppose I feel closer to this than to Delacroix. A higher style. Talk about noblesse! The landscape on the easel is like a collage and yet it can't be taken out."

The great horizontal bar of cliff crushing the mourners of THE BURIAL AT ORNANS:

"A friend once invited us to a weekend in the country. It was a great site. There was some land available nearby and we talked about buying it. Then, next morning, I woke up saying: Impossible, we can't live here, there are rocks behind the house. It would have been like working with a Courbet behind me."

Today at least, Courbet is Newman's painter.

"It has to do with the so-called static quality in Courbet against the turbulence in Delacroix and Géricault. They are related to De Kooning, to Pollock; I am to Courbet. You never tire of him. He is so quiet."

"Something to do with the colossal size?"

"The size is nothing; what matters is the scale."

We turn the corner at the other end of the gallery. The heroic dimensions of the *grandes machines* give way to the modest formats of the Beistegui Collection. Newman takes up the monocle that dangles on his chest to examine one of these canvases. A guard pounces on him.

"It's forbidden!"

"What's forbidden?"

"Magnifying glasses."

"But this is a looking glass."

"All the same, you might set fire to something by

capturing the sun's rays."

"But it's raining."

Indeed, darkness is growing by the minute. We return to the large gallery. No light but that which falls through the glass ceiling; on this sooty December mid-afternoon, it is plunged into what one might euphemistically call a deep penumbra. A few visitors glide by us, apparently unperturbed by the fact that they cannot see the paintings: their ears pressed against audio devices that dispense explanations, they do not see the pictures, they hear them. Newman, too, is unperturbed by the darkness.

"It doesn't matter. A picture is like a person: you sense them even in bad light."

Darkness removes what distinguishes the concerns of a Géricault—the rhetoric, for instance, that side of him that belongs to his time—from his own.

"I remember walking into the National Gallery in Washington and suddenly seeing the Rembrandts—all that brown, with a streak of light coming down the middle—as my own painting."

Night has released, like so many owls unblinded, the immutable presence of works separated by history: the Huron who hides within every Franz Josef awakens:

"I feel related to this, to the past. If I am talking to anyone, I am talking to Michelangelo. The great guys are concerned with the same problems."

"Namely?"

"Saying something about life and about man and about himself: that's what a painter is about. Otherwise he is a pattern-maker. That's why I am unsympathetic to Mohammedan art."

The darkness that descends upon the Louvre sheds light on what Barnett Newman's work is about. It provides a kind of meteorological equivalent of the reductive process that has made painting abstract; retro-

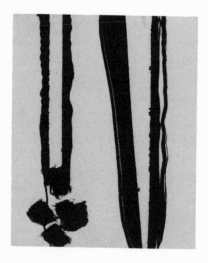

actively, it submits past painting to the "negative theology" (the theology which, by stating what God is not,
rather than what he is, eliminates qualificatives that are
actually petty restrictions on His infinity) that has
stripped modern painting to the essential. Past art thus
becomes modern, present. And the essence disclosed is
what, at any time, constitutes the real present: the
present is permanent.

What the negative theology eliminates is, of course,
anecdote. But what is the essence which its removal lays
bare? This, too, would seem obvious: the work's structure. Silence the biblical tale told by WEDDING FEAST AT
CANA and what you have is a pattern of triangles and
circles. As the tide of subject matter recedes, geometry
emerges. And so one might indeed suppose by looking
at Newman's work.

But that would be forgetting the Huron inside Franz
Josef: Newman's idiom may be borrowed from *esprit
de géometrie,* but the message is delivered by *esprit de
finesse.* He has no sympathy for pattern-making,
whether it be Muslim decoration or industrial aesthetics. And the only antidote to pattern-making is subject
matter. *"The central issue of painting is the subject*

matter," he once wrote. A sentence recurs frequently in his conversation: *"Our problem, today, is* what *to paint."* It is a problem, for the reductive process that constitutes the history of modern painting has brutally shown up the distinction between manifest anecdote and underlying structure. A distinction so basic imposes, sooner or later, a choice: once you are aware that *before* being a battle horse or a Madonna, a picture is made of lines and colors, arranged in a certain order —as Maurice Denis' famous formula puts it—it becomes very difficult to believe that these lines and colors can be a battle horse or a Madonna at all. Subject matter and pattern are contradictory, the modern painter knows. Hence for someone who accepts this fact, as Newman does, the problem of what to paint would appear insoluble.

Newman, however, does not accept the contradiction. He welcomes the elimination of the overt subject matter because it reveals not the pattern but the real subject—*"the high subject,"* as he says. For Newman, the structure *is* the subject. Or rather it becomes the subject in the special light that Newman throws upon it. A circle, according to how one looks at it, may be a formula $(\pi 2R^2)$, a symbol of divine perfection or (as in Tantra) a mystical experience. Geometry is turned into subject by *"passion"* (one of Newman's favorite words). It is precisely because the pattern freezes so easily into pat formula or symbol that it must be revived by the immediacy of experience. In this sense, Newman's work is closely related to action painting: it is not planned, but immediate.

Unlike it, however, Newman's experience is metaphysical rather than physical. Strangely, the words in the Book of Kells which he mistook for his initials said: "In the beginning. . . ." It is only the experience of the beginning that abolishes the distinction between visual and ideal, between pattern and subject.

Newman's originality consists in striving for originality in its original sense: a return to the origins. His interest in surrealism is explained by the yearning for the initial: depth psychology reaches into older, earlier layers of the psyche. His concern with primitive art also relates to his fascination with firstness. Yet primitivism, like surrealism, remain in the realm of the anecdotal. Newman's contention is far more radical. *"The first man was an artist,"* he has written. To work as an artist is therefore to find one's way back to the source. *"What is the raison d'être, what is the explanation of the seemingly insane drive of man to be painter and poet if it is not an act of defiance against man's fall and an assertion that he return to the Adam of the Garden of Eden? For the artists are the first men."* Not action painting, then, but painting as act, for it is in the act of painting that the firstness lies.

Why? Because Adam himself—or better, his awareness of himself—is the first painting: a finite, erect figure against an endless background, "a false note in the divine harmony," in Baudelaire's words. The second painting reproduces the awareness of this tragic asymmetry: a finite line drawn on an endless ground. It is the original subject, and it remains the permanent subject beneath the anecdotal pretexts. Such pretexts, by guiding us toward illusion, narrative, description, culture, distract us from the only thing that makes art meaningful, for only the simple, physical act of affirming the irreducible distinction of finite line and endless space reproduces the basic human situation.

Adam's awareness of his identity entails his exile from the womb of wholeness, from Eden. The line divides. Newman's continuous demand for *"totality"* stems from the fact that the act of painting—the drawing of the line—is an act of disruption, of destruction of totality. Yet the same act is entrusted with the task of restoring totality. To achieve this, the artist must

assert his ability to reproduce a drawing of the line still
earlier than first man's: the act by which God created
the world. Was the act of creation not literally a drawing of the line between darkness and light, water and
earth, etc.? The line, then, is the spine around which
life orders itself symmetrically. In the final resort, the
painting is a field defined by the interreactions of those
two lines—positive and negative, symmetric and asym-
metric—which sometimes coincide, sometimes move
apart in extreme tension. At times the one echoes the
other like an ominous *doppelgänger;* at others, the first
is trenchant while its double is still enrobed in wisps of
hesitancy, as if to diffract the ambivalence of the essential act. The work is a re-enactment of the metaphysical plight of man. The form is the content, the
sign is the meaning; pure, abstract idea and concrete,
aesthetic gesture are one, but only at the moment of
firstness.

And the resurrection of firstness is precisely what the
nature of modern painting has made possible. The

three-dimensionality elaborated by the Renaissance built an artificial room isolated from real space, a cave in which it gathered its phantoms, staged its ghost dramas. The reinvention of flatness destroyed the ghetto, exposed the canvas as a simple fragment of real space and the images on it as mere traces of pencil or pigment. Perspective is the dimension of memory: flatness walled up memory's avenues, forced painters to work in the here-and-now. Flatness is the necessary physical prerequisite of firstness.

But it is not sufficient. Moral awareness is needed. *"I have no interest in the 'finished' picture,"* Newman writes. The *"sublime"* is his concern, not *"perfection."* The point is not to make a flat picture, but to repeat, with the help of flatness, the original act of painting. To achieve this, the artist must treat his canvas as if it were part of space as a whole. The crucial notion here is *"scale,"* as opposed to *"size"* or *"dimension."* Scale is an attribute of total space, or rather of images, forms that take up the heroic, hopeless challenge of pitting themselves against total space. Size, on the other hand, is an attribute of the canvas and of the forms that relate themselves to its limits. The high subject alone—the act of painting—can have scale: dimensional work generates anecdotes or patterns. Scale is always big; size, always small. Since he uses a piece of canvas for his work, the painter necessarily begins with the data of dimension. His work becomes art only if he succeeds in turning size into scale, into event, into the one event that the act of painting can reproduce: man's presence in the world.

The motor of the conversion of size into scale is *"high passion,"* intellectual postulation, belief. These, one might object, fall outside the scope of the visible. But of two gods, the one believed in works visible wonders. The ultimate test of the existence of Newman's painting as a *cosa mentale* is their communicability to another person's mind. These pages present such a test. Will he recognize himself? Distance has made me almost as unfamiliar with his work as he was with the Louvre.

Well, perhaps not quite. For, as I learned in the course of our walks, behind every real painting in the Louvre lurks a Barnett Newman.

Index

Pierre Schneider

Pierre Schneider was born in Antwerp, Belgium, in 1925. He earned his bachelor's degree at the University of California at Berkeley and his Ph.D. at Harvard, where he was a Junior Fellow in the Society of Fellows from 1947 to 1950. Since then he has been living in Paris, where he is currently art editor of the weekly news magazine *L'Express*.

Among his previous books are *La Voix Vive* (1953), a collection of essays on art and literature; *Les Cinq Saisons* (1955), essays ranging from the poetic to the philosophic; *Jules Renard* (1956), a study of Renard and his time; *L'Unique Source* (1959), a book of dialogues similar in form to this work; and *Le Voir et le savoir* (1964), an essay on Nicolas Poussin. He also edited a critical edition of the works of Charles Baudelaire, and on the centennial of the latter's death he organized a colloquium in Paris of leading artists, poets, critics and historians, whose collected papers have been published in several languages.

In English, M. Schneider has published *The World of Watteau* and *The World of Manet* in the Time-Life Art Library. He is currently at work on a major critical biography of Henri Matisse and was responsible for the centennial exhibition of Matisse's work held in 1970 at the Grand Palais in Paris. He has published numerous essays and articles in art and literary magazines in Europe, Latin America, the United States and Japan. Formerly Paris editor of *Art News*, he has recently contributed a monthly column on French culture to *The New York Times*. For the past three years, he has produced a series of art films for French television.